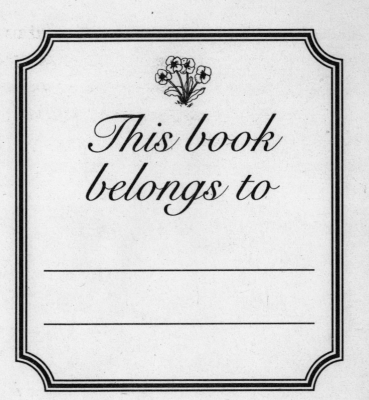

This book belongs to

_____

_____

Best Loved
FAIRYLAND
TALES

Best Loved
FAIRYLAND
TALES

SIENA

THIS IS A SIENA BOOK

SIENA is an imprint of PARRAGON

Parragon
13 Whiteladies Road
Clifton
Bristol BS8 1PB

Copyright © Parragon 1999

ISBN 0-75253-010-0

Printed in Great Britain

Designed by Mik Martin
Cover illustration by Terry Rogers

CONTENTS

Granny Casts a Spell

SUSIE WAS very fond of her Granny. Each day, when Susie got home from school, Granny was always there sitting by the fire knitting. Granny knitted so fast that sometimes it seemed as though the knitting needles sparked in the firelight.

"Do you know," Granny would say, "that I'm really a witch?" Susie always laughed when Granny said that because she didn't look at all like a witch. She had a smiling face and kind eyes and she never wore black. Not ever. When Granny wasn't looking, Susie would take a peek inside her wardrobe just in case she might find a broomstick or a witch's hat. But she never found so much as a book of spells.

"I don't believe you're a witch," said Susie.

"I am," replied Granny, "and I'll cast a spell one day. You'll know when that day comes, for my needles will start to knit by themselves." After that, Susie kept a careful watch over Granny's needles, but they always lay quite still in the basket of knitting.

One day, Susie was playing in her garden when she heard the sound of weeping. The sound seemed to be coming from under the old tree in the corner. She walked towards the tree and as she did so the crying noise got louder, but she could not see anyone there. Then she looked down at her feet and there — sitting on a mossy stone — was a tiny little man. He was neatly dressed in a yellow velvet waistcoat and knickerbockers. On his feet were beautiful, shiny, buckled shoes, and a three-cornered hat with a wren's feather in it trembled on his shaking head. When the little man saw Susie, he stopped crying and started to dab his eyes with a fine lace handkerchief.

"Whatever can the matter be?" asked Susie, crouching down.

"Oh dear, oh dear!" sobbed the little man, "I am the fairy princess's tailor and she has asked me to make

her a lovely gown to wear to the
May Ball tonight, but a wicked elf
has played a trick on me and turned
all my fine gossamer fabric into bats'
wings. Now I shall never be able to
make the princess's gown and she
will be very angry with me." He
started to cry again.

"Don't cry!" said Susie. "I'm
sure I can help. My Granny's got a

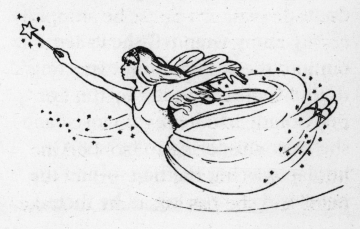

sewing basket full of odds and ends. I'll see if she's got anything nice for a party dress. I'm sure she won't mind sparing some — after all, you won't need much," she said. At that, the little man looked a bit more cheerful.

"Wait here," said Susie, "while I run indoors and see." She ran up the garden path and in through the back door.

"Granny, Granny!" she called. She ran into the sitting room expecting to find Granny knitting by the fire. But Granny had her eyes closed and she was whispering to herself. On her lap was her knitting — and the needles were moving all by themselves, so that the yarn danced up and down on the old lady's knees.

For a moment, Susie was too astounded to move. Then she thought, "I hope Granny's not casting a bad spell. I'd better make sure the little tailor is alright."

She ran back down the garden path and there under the tree sat the tailor, surrounded by a great pile of gorgeous gossamer, shining in the sunlight.

"I've never seen such fine material — ever!" he exclaimed. "But where did it come from? I just closed my eyes to dab them with my hanky and when I opened them again — there it was!"

"I don't know," said Susie, "but I think my Granny might have had something to do with it."

"Well, I'd never be able to thank her enough," said the tailor. "For now I shall be able to make the finest gown in the whole of fairyland. The princess will dance the night away in the prettiest dress there ever was." He paused and then went on, "I'm

also indebted to you, for it was you who helped me in the first place. I would like it very much if you came to the May Ball, too."

"Why, thank you so much," Susie replied, "I should like that very much." She didn't want to hurt the tailor's feelings but she knew she couldn't go — she was far too big to go to a fairy ball!

"Well I must get on with the dress now," said the little man, reaching for a pair of fairy scissors. "See you tonight!" And with that he vanished.

Susie went indoors again. Granny was knitting by the fire as usual. Susie wondered if she had dreamed the whole thing. Everything seemed so normal. Really, how could she have imagined she'd seen a fairy tailor in the garden! And as for Granny casting a spell!

That night, Susie lay in bed and wondered if the fairies really were having a ball. How she longed to be there! Once she thought she heard a tapping at the window. Was that the fairy tailor she saw through the glass — or was she imagining it? In the middle of the night she awoke with a start. There was a click, clicking noise at the end of her bed.

"Granny is that you?" called Susie.

"Yes, dear," replied Granny. "I

couldn't sleep, so I decided to do some knitting. All at once the needles started twitching, so I knew it was time to cast a spell. What is your wish, Susie?"

"I... I...," stammered Susie, "I want to go to the May Ball," she blurted.

"Then you shall, my dear," said Granny.

In an instant, Susie felt herself

shrinking and when she looked down she saw she was wearing a beautiful gown and tiny satin slippers. Then she floated on gossamer wings out through the window and off to the Ball.

The next morning, Susie woke up in her bed. Had it all been a dream — the revelry, the fairy food, the frog band, the dance with the fairy prince? Then she saw something peeping out from under her pillow. And what do you think it was? It was a tiny, tiny shred of the finest gossamer fabric.

Peter Meets a Dragon

ONCE UPON A TIME there was a young boy named Peter. He lived in an ordinary house with an ordinary Mum and Dad, an ordinary sister and an ordinary pet cat, called Jasper. In fact, everything in Peter's life was so ordinary that he sometimes wished that something extraordinary would happen. "Why doesn't a giant come and squash the house flat with his foot?" he wondered, and "If only a pirate would take my sister hostage!" But each day, Peter would wake up in the morning and everything was just the same as it had been the day before.

One morning Peter woke up to find a very strange smell in the house. Looking out of his bedroom window, he saw that the front lawn was scorched and blackened. There was smoke drifting off the grass and, further away, he could see some bushes ablaze.

Peter rushed downstairs and out of the front door. He ran out of the garden and down the lane following the trail of smoke and burning grass. He grew more and more puzzled, however, as there was no sign of anything that could have caused such a blaze.

Peter was about to run home and tell his Mum and Dad, when he heard a panting noise coming from the undergrowth. Parting the bushes gently with his hands he found a young creature. It had green, scaly skin, a pair of wings and a long snout full of sharp teeth. Every now and again a little tongue of flame came from its nostrils, setting the grass around it on fire. "A baby dragon!" Peter said to himself, in great surprise. Big tears were rolling out of the dragon's yellow eyes and down its scaly cheeks as it flapped its wings desperately and tried to take off.

When the dragon saw Peter it stopped flapping its wings.

"Oh, woe is me!" it sobbed. "Where am I?"

"Where do you want to be?"

asked Peter, kneeling down on the scorched ground.

"I want to be in Dragonland with my friends," replied the dragon. "We were all flying together, but I just couldn't keep up with them. I got tired and needed a rest. I called to the others but they didn't hear me. Then I just had to stop and get my breath back. Now I don't know where I am, or if I'll ever see my

friends again!" And with that the baby dragon started to cry once more.

"I'm sure I can help. I'll get you home," said Peter, though he had no idea how.

"You?" hissed a voice nearby. "How could you possibly help? You're just a boy!" Peter looked round, and to his astonishment found Jasper sitting behind him. "I suppose you're going to wave a magic wand, are you?" continued Jasper. "You need to call in an expert." Then he turned his back on Peter and the baby dragon and started washing his paws.

Peter was astounded. He'd never

heard Jasper talking before. He had thought he was just an ordinary pet cat. "W… w… what do you mean?" he stammered.

"Well," said Jasper, glancing over his shoulder at Peter, "I reckon that horse over there could help. Follow me."

So Peter and the baby dragon — whose name was Flame — followed Jasper over to where the horse stood at the edge of a field. Jasper leaped up on to the gate and called to the horse. Then he whispered in the horse's ear. The horse thought for a moment, then whispered back in Jasper's ear.

"He says he's got a friend on the

other side of the wood who'll help," said Jasper.

"But how?" said Peter, looking perplexed.

"Be patient! Follow me!" said Jasper as he stalked off through the grass. "And tell your friend to stop setting fire to everything!" he added. Peter saw, to his horror, that Flame was indeed blazing a trail through the field.

"I can't help it," cried Flame, about to burst into tears again. "Every time I get out of breath I start to pant, and then I start breathing fire."

"Let me carry you," said Peter. He picked Flame up in his arms and ran after Jasper. The baby dragon felt very strange. His body was all cold and clammy, but his mouth was still breathing hot smoke, which made Peter's eyes water.

He ran through the wood, just keeping Jasper's upright tail in sight. On the other side of the wood was another field, and in the field was a horse. But this was no ordinary horse. Peter stopped dead in his tracks and stared. The horse was pure milky white, and from its head grew a single, long horn. "A unicorn!" breathed Peter.

Jasper was already talking to the unicorn. He beckoned with his paw to Peter. "He'll take your friend home and you can go, too, Peter, but don't be late for tea, or you know what your mother will say." And with that, Jasper was off.

"Climb aboard," said the unicorn gently.

Peter and the little dragon scrambled up on to the unicorn's back. "What an adventure," thought Peter. Up, up, and away they soared through the clouds.

Flame held tightly on to Peter's hand with his clammy paw. At last Peter could see a mountain ahead through the clouds. Now they were descending through the clouds again, and soon the unicorn landed right at the top of the mountain. "I'm home!" squeaked Flame joyously as they landed. Sure enough, several dragons were running over to greet him. They looked quite friendly, but some of them were rather large and one was breathing a great deal of fire.

"Time for me to go," said Peter a little nervously, as Flame jumped off the unicorn's back and flew to the ground. The unicorn took off again and soon they were back in the field once more.

As he slid off the unicorn's back, Peter turned to thank him, but when he looked he saw that it was just an ordinary horse with no trace of a horn at all. Peter walked back home across the field, but there was no sign of burnt grass. He reached his own front lawn, which was also in perfect condition. Peter felt more and more perplexed. "I hope Jasper can explain," he thought, as the cat ran past him and into the house.

"Jasper, I took the baby dragon home. What's happened to the burnt grass?" he blurted out. But Jasper said not a word. He ignored Peter and curled up in his basket.

When Peter wasn't looking, however, Jasper gave him a glance that seemed to say, "Well, was that a big enough adventure for you?"

The Enchanted Harp

LONG AGO there lived a pedlar. Every day he took up the same place in the market square with his harp. Now this was no ordinary harp. It was an enchanted harp. The pedlar would call out to passers-by and, for a penny, the harp would play all on its own any tune they wished. It could play any sort of tune from the slowest, most tearful ballad to the liveliest, happiest jig. It could play music for any occasion. Sometimes a wedding party would come by just to have the harp play a tune for the bride and groom.

Now one day a young man passed through the town. He heard the sound of the harp's sweet music coming from the market square and made his way over to where the pedlar stood. He couldn't believe his eyes or his ears! The harp was playing a lullaby for a lady with a baby that was crying. The music was so enchanting that the baby soon stopped wailing and was fast asleep. Then he saw an old man give the pedlar a penny and whisper in his ear. The harp changed its tune and now it played an ancient melody that the old man had not heard for many a year, and his eyes filled with tears of gratitude.

The young man watched all this and thought to himself, "If only that harp were mine. I could make a lot more money with it than that silly old pedlar!" He waited a while for the crowd to disperse, and then when he thought no-one was looking he went up to the pedlar and said, "People say that on this day a great spotted pig will fall out of the sky and land on the market square. Keep a look out and if you see a pair of trotters in the sky, get out of the way fast!" And he pointed up at the sky. The pedlar peered upwards but all he could see were scudding white clouds.

While he was staring up, the young man snatched the harp and was out of the market square and away down the street before the pedlar realised what had happened.

"Stop! Thief!" the pedlar shouted. But it was too late. By the time folk gave chase the young man had gone. He didn't stop running until he reached a town many miles away, where no-one had seen the enchanted harp before.

The young man set up the harp and called out to passers-by, "Two pennies and my harp will play any tune you wish!" A man and woman came up and asked for a waltz and, sure enough, the harp began to play. The couple spun round the square merrily and were happy enough to give the young man two pennies.

More and more people came by and asked for tunes. The young man rubbed his hands with pleasure. "I shall surely make my fortune now," he said to himself.

Weeks passed and the young man did, indeed, make a lot of money. He didn't care at all how much he charged. If someone who looked wealthy came along he might charge them six pennies or even eight. By now he had completely forgotten that he had stolen the harp and that it didn't belong to him at all. He bought himself fine clothes and ate expensive food and generally considered himself rather clever.

Then one day an old man in a

broad-brimmed hat came past and asked for a tune. He grumbled a bit when the young man asked for two pennies but held out the coins, making sure the young man could not see his face — for he was the pedlar!

"I'd like the harp to play a tune to drive you mad," said the old man.

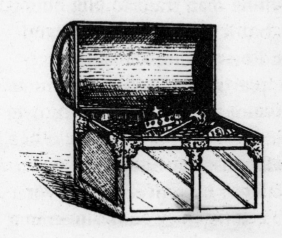

The young man thought this was a strange request but he had taken the coins and the harp had already started to play. It played a short and very silly tune. Then it played it again. And again. And again. And again. It simply wouldn't stop. By now the old man had slipped away, so when people weren't watching the young man tried to kick the harp, but it side-stepped him and carried on playing. On and on it went, playing that infuriating tune. The young man put his hands over his ears to block out the noise, but the harp just played louder.

Passers-by moved away. "What a terrible tune," they said. The young man tried to move away, too, but the harp just followed him down the road, still playing.

Everywhere he went, night and day, the harp followed the young man until he was at his wits' end. He had used up all his money and he was in despair. Finally, he thought there was only one thing to do. He must go back to the pedlar and beg him to stop the harp.

It took him a while to make his way back to the town where the pedlar lived, but sure enough there he was, standing in the market square trying to sell a few old pots and pans to passers-by. He looked very unhappy, and the young man

felt truly sorry for what he had done.

He approached the pedlar with the harp still playing away behind him. He was about to explain when, to his surprise, the pedlar stopped him and said, "I know all about your plight. I will stop the harp playing its maddening tune on one condition."

"I'll do anything," said the young man.

"You must ask people what tune they would liked played and then you must give them a penny each time."

The young man gratefully agreed and the pedlar told the harp to stop playing. The young man had to work very hard to earn enough money to give people their pennies, but he was willing to do so in return for the pedlar making the harp stop playing that maddening tune!

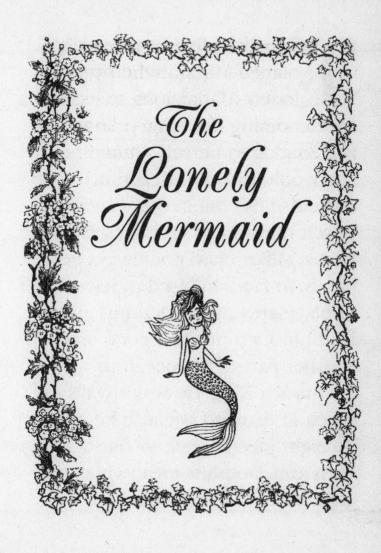

The Lonely Mermaid

THERE ONCE lived a mermaid named Miriam who was very lonely. All day long she sat on a rock combing her long, yellow hair and singing to herself. Sometimes she would flick her beautiful turquoise fish tail in the water and watch the ripples spreading far out to sea. Miriam had not always been lonely. In fact, she used to have a pair of playmates called Octopus and Dolphin. Octopus had gone off to another part of the ocean to work for the Sea King. He was always much in demand because he could do eight jobs at once — one with each arm. Dolphin, meanwhile, had gone away to teach singing in a school of dolphins. Miriam once thought she heard his lovely song far away across the ocean and she hoped in vain that he might come back and play.

One day Miriam was sitting on her favourite rock as usual. "How lonely I am," she sighed to her

reflection as she combed her hair and gazed at herself in the mirror.

To her astonishment, her reflection seemed to answer back. "Don't be lonely," said a voice. "Come and play with me."

Miriam couldn't understand it at all. She peered into the mirror and then she saw, beyond her own reflection, another mermaid! She was so startled that she dropped the mirror and her comb and spun around.

Miriam was puzzled by the sight in front of her. For there, sitting on the next rock was another mermaid — and yet she didn't look like a mermaid in many ways. She had

short, dark, curly hair and wore a
strange costume that definitely
wasn't made of seaweed. When
Miriam looked down to where the
mermaid's fish tail should have been,
she wanted to burst out laughing.

For instead of a beautiful tail, the

other mermaid had two strange limbs like an extra long pair of arms stretching down.

The other 'mermaid', who was really a little girl called Georgie, was equally amazed by the sight of Miriam. She had seen pictures of mermaids in books before, but now she couldn't quite believe her eyes. For here, on the rock beside her, was a real live mermaid!

For a moment they were both too astonished to speak. Then they both said at once, "Who are you?"

"I'm Miriam," said Miriam.

"I'm Georgie," said Georgie.

"Let's go for a swim," said Miriam. Soon the two of them were in the water, chasing each other and giggling.

"Let's play tag along the beach," suggested Georgie, and started swimming towards the shore. She had quite forgotten that Miriam would not be able to run around on dry land. Miriam followed though she was rather afraid, as her mother had always told her not to go near the shore in case she got stranded. Georgie ran out of the water and up on to the beach.

"Wait for me!" called Miriam, struggling in the water as her tail thrashed about. Then, to her astonishment, something strange happened. She found she could leave the water with ease and, looking down, saw that her tail had disappeared and that in its place were two of those strange long arm things like Georgie's.

"What's happened?" she wailed.

Georgie looked round. "You've grown legs!" she shouted in amazement. "Now you can play tag!"

Miriam found that she rather liked having legs. She tried jumping in the air, and Georgie taught her to hop and skip. "You can come and stay at my house, but first I must find you some clothes," said Georgie, looking at Miriam who was wearing nothing but her long, yellow hair. "Wait for me here!"

Georgie ran off and soon she was back with a tee shirt and shorts. Miriam put them on. They ran back to Georgie's house together. "This is my friend Miriam," said Georgie to her mother. "Can she stay for tea?"

"Why, of course," said Georgie's mother.

"What's that strange thing?" whispered Miriam.

"It's a chair," said Georgie. She showed Miriam how to sit on the chair. All through teatime Miriam watched Georgie to see how she should eat from a plate and drink from a cup and saucer. She'd never tasted food like this before. How she wished she could have chocolate cake at home under the sea!

After tea Miriam said, "Now I'll show you how to do something." Taking Georgie by the hand she led her down to the beach again. There they picked up shells, and then Miriam showed Georgie how to make a lovely necklace from shells threaded with seaweed. While they made their necklaces, Miriam taught Georgie how to sing songs of the sea.

Soon it was bedtime. "You can sleep in the spare bed in my room," said Georgie. Miriam slipped in between the sheets. How strange it felt! She was used to feeling water

all around her and here she was
lying in a bed. She tossed and
turned, feeling hotter and hotter, and
couldn't sleep at all. In the middle of
the night she got up and threw open
the window to get some fresh air.
She could smell the salty sea air and
she began to feel rather homesick.
Then she heard a familiar sound
from far away. It was Dolphin calling
to her! The noise was getting closer
and closer until at last Miriam knew
what she must do. She slipped out of
the house and ran down to the
beach in the moonlight. As soon as
her toes touched the water, her legs
turned back into a fish tail and she
swam out to sea to join Dolphin.

The next morning, when Georgie woke up, she was very upset to find that her friend had gone. When she told her mother who Miriam really was, her mother said, "The sea is a mermaid's true home and that's where she belongs. But I'm sure you two will always be friends."

And indeed, from time to time, Georgie was sure that she could see Miriam waving to her from the sea.

The Mirror of Dreams

THE HOUSE on the corner of Nightingale Avenue was tall and very handsome, and was by far the largest in the neighbourhood. From the street you could see four floors of beautifully decorated rooms, and if you peeped over the railings you could see the basement below.

If you were lucky enough to be asked into the house, and passed through the beautiful hallways into the playroom, you might meet the owner's daughter, Cordelia.

Sometimes Cordelia would be sitting in her silk pyjamas playing on her grand piano, and sometimes she would be dressed in the finest

velvet gowns playing with her lovely dolls.

If you went down the stairs and
into the basement, you might come
across Polly. Polly's mother was a
chambermaid in the house, and
worked hard all day long to make
the house sparkling clean. Sometimes Polly helped her to polish the
ornaments and dust the furniture,
but more often Polly sat on her own
in her small bedroom drawing
pictures with some crayons on a
drawing pad she had been given for
her birthday. When Polly was helping
to polish the furniture she would
look longingly at all of Cordelia's fine
clothes and toys, and when she sat

alone in her room she would draw pictures of all the beautiful things she would like to own if only she could afford them.

One day, a large parcel was delivered to the house and taken upstairs to Cordelia's bedroom. A little while later, Cordelia's maid carried a pretty, ornate mirror down from her room and put it with the rubbish waiting for collection outside the house. Polly asked the maid why the mirror was to be thrown away, and the maid explained that Cordelia had been given a new mirror in which to brush her long, silky locks, and that she didn't need it any more. The maid then asked if Polly would like the old mirror, and of course Polly accepted with pleasure — it was the most beautiful thing she had ever owned.

Polly carried the mirror back to her room and polished it lovingly. As she polished the glass a strange thing started to happen. The glass went misty, and then cleared as her own reflection stared back at her once more. But the reflection that stared back was not dressed in rags and worn old clothes as Polly was, but in a rich gown of the most beautiful cream satin, with pink bows and apricot lace.

Polly was entranced. She looked almost as beautiful as Cordelia! Her hair gleamed and her fingers were white and magnificent. As she looked further into the mirror, she saw herself dancing at a ball, and then sitting down to eat the finest food she had ever seen — hams and roasted meats, and cakes of strawberries and cream!

And then the mirror spoke to her. "I am the Mirror of Dreams," the cool, clear voice said. "Whatever your heart desires most will be reflected in my shiny surface."

Polly was astounded, but so happy. She didn't care that it was only a day dream, for when she saw her reflection in the beautiful clothes, she felt as if she were truly there dancing and eating the fine foods — she could almost taste the fruit and cream in her mouth!

From that day on, Polly sat in

her room every day, and dreamed and dreamed and dreamed. She had never felt so happy before, and could not wait to wake up each morning to visit her imaginary world. She certainly didn't understand how Cordelia could have thrown away such a magical wonder, and thought that she could not have known of its enchanting secret. She supposed also that Cordelia could have had no use for such a mirror, for whatever Cordelia wanted in real life she received, and would have no need to dream. But Polly was to find out that this was very far from true!

Weeks passed, and every day Polly sat and dreamed of ermine

cloaks, of diamonds and pearls, of
parties and picnics and carnivals.
Eventually, she had dreamed every
dream she had ever wanted. And
Polly began to realise that it no
longer made her as happy as it once
had, and she began to grow weary of
her Mirror of Dreams. She sat in
front of the mirror less and less, and
eventually when she did visit the
mirror she could not think of a
single thing that would make her
happy. Even the dreams she had in
which her mother wore fine silk
clothes and didn't have to scrub and
clean for their living could no longer
make her happy.

She preferred her real mother,

who came to kiss her good night and read her stories no matter how tired and overworked she was. Eventually she stopped looking in the mirror altogether, and finally decided to throw the mirror away — it had only made her more unhappy.

As the long winter turned into spring she acted upon her decision, and took down the mirror to throw away with the rubbish. But as she looked into the glass, it misted over in its familiar way and she saw herself in the mirror as she looked in real life, but in it she was playing with other children like herself, and reading stories with them and sharing toys. She felt gloriously happy, and knew in that instant that all she wanted was a very good friend. She realised in that moment, too, that perhaps Cordelia really had known the mirror's secret, but that she also had become more unhappy as the dreams faded and reality forced itself upon her. She wondered aloud what it was that Cordelia had dreamed of, and for the second and last time the mirror spoke in its cool, clear voice.

"The Mirror of Dreams showed Cordelia her heart's desire, and her heart desires a true friend and companion — someone who is not jealous of her wealth, but a friend who will share her hopes and dreams, and with whom she can have parties, games and picnics."

Polly put the mirror down and thought with amazement that she could be that friend, if Cordelia would be friends with someone poor but honest and true. Polly left the mirror with the household rubbish and was about to make the descent back to the basement, when she saw Cordelia standing in the garden at the back of the house. Cordelia had seen her discard the mirror, and shyly walked up to Polly. Polly overcame her shyness also and went to meet Cordelia, and then she told her they shared the same dream.

Cordelia and Polly became the best of friends from that day on. They shared everything they had, no matter how much or little. They talked and laughed together all day long, and they played long into the evening. They didn't have to dream any more, for they had both got their true heart's desire.

The Giant Who Shrank

ONCE UPON A TIME in a far-off land, there lived a huge giant. He made his home in a big cave high up in the mountains. His bed, table and chairs were made from great tree trunks. And when he wanted a drink, he simply filled an old bath tub with water and drank it down in one enormous gulp. When he snored — which he did almost every night — it sounded like a huge thunderstorm, and the noise echoed all around the mountains.

At the bottom of the mountains there was a village, but all the folk in the village were very different from the giant, for they were not big at all. They were just like you and me.

They were afraid of the giant, of course, and whenever he came striding down the mountains to hunt, they all ran away into the woods or locked themselves inside their houses. Sometimes, the clumsy giant would tramp around the village squashing houses with his great feet as he went, and that only made the village folk even more frightened of him!

Although the giant was so big and strong, he was not a bad giant, but he was very, very lonely because everyone ran away whenever he appeared. Sometimes, while he was sitting alone in his cave, he could hear the villagers having feasts and parties and he longed to join them and be just like them.

One day, when the giant was tramping around the village as usual, something glinting in the sun caught his eye. At the top of a big tree (which of course was not very big as far as the giant was concerned) lay a gold box.

The giant bent down and picked up the box. To his surprise he heard a small voice inside say, "Help! Help! Let me out!"

The giant opened the box and out jumped an elf. "Thank you, thank you, large sir," he said. "I am a magic elf, but one of my spells went wrong and I got locked inside this box. No-one in the village could hear me calling for help high up in this tree."

To show his thanks, the elf said he would grant the giant one wish.

"I wish I could be the same as all the other villagers," boomed the giant.

"What a difficult wish," said the elf. "You are so big! But I will do my best."

The elf closed his eyes and chanted a magic spell. But nothing seemed to happen — the giant was still as big as ever.

The giant was very sad to discover that he had not shrunk, but he wished the elf well, thanked him for trying and went on his way. As the giant was walking back to his cave in the mountains, he noticed something strange. All the puddles of water that he had passed on the way

down to the village had got bigger.
They were as big as lakes now! The
giant looked up to see if it had been
raining, but the sky was clear and
blue.

Then another strange thing
happened. The big stone steps he
had cut in the mountain side leading

up to his cave had also got bigger! He could hardly clamber up them.

Eventually, puffing and panting, the giant reached the door to his cave. But he could not reach the door knob. It now towered above him, far from his reach.

"What is happening?" thought the giant. "The elf's spell must have gone wrong. Not only am I still a giant, but everything around me has now got even bigger."

Suddenly the truth came to him. Of course! Everything had not become bigger — he had become smaller! The spell had worked after all. Now he was just the same as the other folk in the village.

He made his way to the village, wondering if everyone would still run away as before. But he need not have worried. All the village folk welcomed him into the village, and he lived there happily among them for the rest of his days.

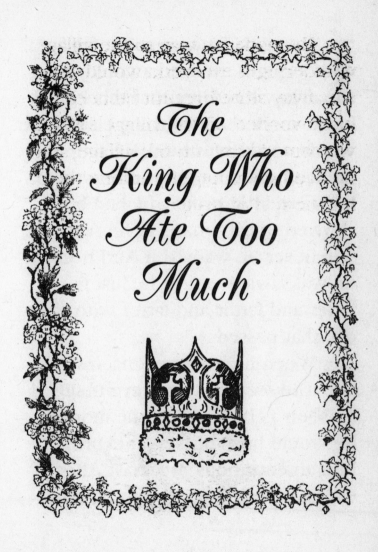

The King Who Ate Too Much

LONG AGO, in a kingdom far, far away, there lived a greedy king. Now the thing that this king loved, more than anything else in the whole world, was food. He simply couldn't get enough of it. Ever since he was a little prince, he had been allowed to eat whatever he wanted, whenever he wanted it. And because he was always eating, he just got fatter and fatter and fatter with every day that passed.

When he became king, his appetite seemed to get even bigger! As soon as he woke in the morning, he would have his servants bring him an enormous breakfast. After eating several huge, steaming bowls of porridge, he would eat slice after slice of hot, buttered toast and jam, followed by all the boiled eggs that the royal chickens could lay.

In case he got a little hungry mid-morning, he would have a snack — usually ten or more chocolate cakes, washed down with as many cups of tea!

At lunchtime, the table would groan with the weight of all the pies, sandwiches, fruit and biscuits that the greedy king was about to gobble down.

For afternoon tea, it would be cakes, cakes and more cakes.

But the king's biggest meal was supper! The royal cooks toiled for most of the day to prepare this feast. When it was time for the king to eat, one servant after another would carry in great bowls of steaming soup, plates of fish of every kind, followed by huge roasts and dishes of vegetables. Down it all went, followed by fruit and jelly. At last, the king would be full and he would retire to his bed for the night.

But the king's greedy eating habits also made him a very thoughtless king. No-one dared tell

him that much of the wealth of the kingdom had to be spent on his huge meals. In the meantime, his loyal subjects were going hungry and becoming poor and needy.

One day, just after the king had eaten his usual big lunch, he began to feel very strange. Not only did he feel even bigger than usual, he also began to feel very light. Suddenly, without any warning, he started floating up from the table and into the air like a big balloon.

"Help! Get me down!" he cried. The royal courtiers and servants jumped up and down and tried in vain to grab the king as he floated upwards, but in no time at all he had floated out of reach. Before anyone knew it, he had floated out of the castle window. Out across the royal grounds he went, over the river and towards the woods and mountains of his kingdom.

"Wooaa-aaah!" cried the king, as he disappeared from view.

Soon, the king began to float over a small farm. He looked down and saw the farmer's children, dressed only in rags, searching for firewood. Some thin, hungry cows stood nearby chewing on a few meagre pieces of hay. Over the next farm he floated, and a similar sad scene met his gaze. Dressed in rags, a poor farmer and his family toiled their soil hoping to grow enough to eat.

Next he floated over a small village. Everywhere he looked he saw shabby, run-down houses in need of repair and people in the streets begging for money.

Every farm and every village the king floated over told the same story of hunger and misery. The king suddenly felt very sad and very ashamed. He had been so busy enjoying himself eating that he hadn't given a thought to the plight of his subjects. While he was getting fatter and fatter, they were all getting thinner and poorer.

Now, a gust of wind was blowing the king back towards his castle. As he was passing over the castle, he suddenly felt himself falling. Down, down, he went until he landed back into the castle grounds with a great thud and a bounce.

That very day, the king sent out a royal proclamation. All his loyal subjects were to come to the castle for a huge feast, after which they would all be given a purse full of gold.

As for the king, he was never greedy again. Instead of spending all his money on food for himself, he gave enough to all the people in the land so that they would never be hungry or poor again.

The Naughty Broom

GOODNESS ME, what a lot of dirt and dust there is all over this kitchen floor," said the maid. She was a very house-proud maid, and didn't like dirt and dust on her floor one little bit. Out came the broom from its place in the cupboard in the corner, and soon the maid was busily sweeping the floor and brushing all the dirt and dust into a big dustpan.

Unfortunately, this kitchen also had elves living in it. They were too tiny to see, of course, but if you upset them they could be very mischievous indeed. As the broom worked away, it swept into one dark corner where the elves were having a party. Suddenly the king elf was swept away from their little table and into the dustpan! The next thing he knew he was being thrown, with all the other rubbish, on to the rubbish tip.

Coughing and spluttering with rage, the king elf finally climbed out from under all the rubbish in the rubbish tip and stood on top of it. He picked the dirt and dust out of his ears and nose, pulled a fish bone from out of his trousers and tried to look as king-like as he could, having just been thrown on to a rubbish tip. "Who did this?" he squeaked at the top of his voice. "I'll make someone very, very sorry indeed," he vowed.

Eventually he made his way back to the house, and into the kitchen again. The other elves looked at the king elf and did their best not to laugh. For the king elf was still looking very dirty and untidy, and still had bits of rubbish stuck all over him. But the other elves knew better than to laugh at the king, because he was likely to cast a bad spell on them if they did.

"It was the broom that did it," chorused all the other elves.

"Right," said the king elf, "then I'm going to cast a bad spell on the broom."

The broom was by now back in its cupboard. The king elf marched

over to the cupboard and jumped in
through the keyhole. The king elf
pointed to the broom and said,
   "Bubble, bubble, gubble, gubble,
   Go and cause a lot of trouble!"
And with that the broom suddenly
stood to attention, its bristles
quivering. It was night time now and
everyone in the house was asleep.
The broom opened its cupboard
door and sprang into the kitchen. It
then unlocked the kitchen door and
went outside. Straight to the rubbish
tip it went, and with a flick of its
bristles, swept a huge pile of rubbish
back into the kitchen. Tin cans, dirt,
dust, chicken bones and goodness
knows what else all got swept on to

the kitchen floor. The broom then closed the kitchen door, took itself back to its cupboard and all was quiet until morning.

When the maid came down into the kitchen, she couldn't believe her eyes. "Who has made this awful mess?" she said. "If I find out it was those cats . . ." she threatened. She took the broom from the cupboard and swept all the rubbish back outside again.

The next night, the same thing happened. Once it was quiet and everyone in the house was asleep, out of its cupboard came the broom, and into the house came all the rubbish again, swept there as before by the naughty broom. This time, there were fish heads, old bottles and all the soot from the fireplaces.

Well, the maid was speechless. After clearing up again, she got the gardener to burn all the rubbish from the rubbish tip, so that nothing else could be brought in — although she still had no idea how it had happened.

That very night, the naughty broom decided it would make a mess in a different way. So instead of sweeping in rubbish from outside, the broom flew up to the shelves and knocked all the jars to the ground. With a crash they fell to the floor, one after another, and spread their contents everywhere.

"Stop this AT ONCE!" demanded a voice suddenly.

The broom stopped its mischief.

"What do you think you are doing?" said the voice again. The voice had come from a very stern-looking fairy who was now standing on the draining board, with her hands on her hips. What the broom

did not know was that one of the
bottles it had knocked down
contained a good fairy, imprisoned
by the elves. Now she was at last
free, the spell was broken and it was
her turn to cast a spell.

"Broom, broom, sweep this floor,
Make it cleaner than ever before.
Find the elves that cast your spell,
And sweep them off into the well,"
she chanted.

The broom went to work. It
seemed to sweep so fast that its
bristles just became a blur. Into this
corner it went, then into that, and
into every nook and cranny it swept.
Every bit of dirt and dust, and all the
broken bottles, were swept into the

dustpan and then out of the house. Then it came back and swept all the elves down into the well where they couldn't do any more mischief.

In the morning, the maid came down to find a spotlessly clean kitchen. She was puzzled to find some of the jars missing, but between you and me she was also rather pleased. It just meant that there were fewer things to dust.

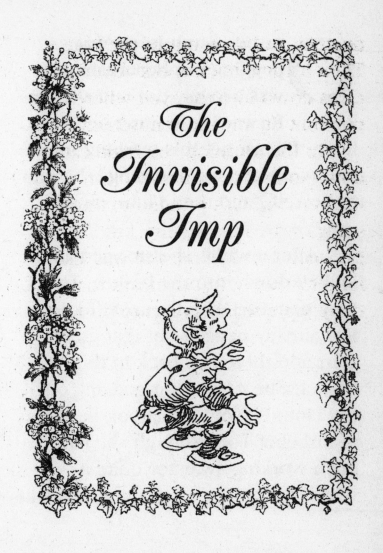

The Invisible Imp

ONE DAY, Sarah Jones was pegging out her washing. It was a lovely day and she was looking forward to visiting her friend Rose. "I'll just get this washing on the line while the sun's shining," she said to herself, "and then I'll be on my way."

After a while, she stopped and looked down into the basket. "That's very peculiar!" she thought. "I know I've already pegged out that green shirt and there it is back in the basket." She carried on pegging out the clothes. Now she shook her head in disbelief. For although she had been working away for quite a while, the basket of washing was still full and there was almost nothing on the line! She began to get quite cross, for she was going to be late getting to Rose's house.

Try as she might, she just could not get that washing pegged. In the end, she had to leave the basket of wet washing and run to Rose's house.

"I'm so sorry I'm late, Rose," she gasped, all out of breath from

running. Sarah told Rose all about what had happened.

"Well," said Rose, "that's a strange coincidence. I was baking some cakes for us to have for tea. Every time I put them in the oven and turned away, they were out of the oven and on the table again! In the end I had to stand guard over them — which reminds me, they were just beginning to cook nicely when you knocked on the door."

The two women went into Rose's kitchen and there were the cakes, sitting on the table again, half-cooked. "Now they're ruined!" cried Rose. "Whatever shall we do?"

At that moment, there was a

noise in the street. Rose and Sarah looked out of the window to see Elmer, the postman, surrounded by a crowd of people all shouting and waving envelopes in the air. The two women ran out into the street. "What's going on?" they cried.

"Elmer's given us all the wrong post," said Rose's neighbour, Dora. "He's normally so reliable, but this morning he seems to have gone completely crazy. Now we've got to sort out all the mail for him."

"I don't know what's happened," wailed Elmer in anguish. "I'm sure I posted all the letters through the right doors."

"Well," said Sarah, "Rose and I

have also found strange things happening to us this morning." She told the crowd their stories. Everyone forgave Elmer when they realised it wasn't his fault, but they were still truly mystified as to what — or who — could have caused all these problems.

But that wasn't the end of it. Oh no, indeed! The butcher's wife served her family mutton stew, but when she lifted the lid the family heard a bleating sound and a little lamb leaped out of the pot. The milkman delivered the milk as usual, but when people took their milk indoors, they found the bottles were full of lemonade. Old Mr Smith tried to pull his chair up to the table and found it was stuck hard to the floor. And when Mrs Smith painted her bedroom blue, she came back and found it had changed to pink with purple spots.

Can you guess what had happened? Do you know who'd been up to all these tricks? It was an imp, of course! The wicked little fellow had become bored playing pranks on the fairies and goblins in fairyland. By now, they knew all his tricks and he was finding it harder and harder to catch them out. Then he had an idea. Why not play tricks in the human world where he would be invisible? So that's exactly what he did. At first, he really only meant to play one or two tricks, but he had such fun that he couldn't resist carrying on.

Well, the invisible imp continued on with his tricks. But of course, as you know, pride comes before a fall, and one day he just went too far. Sarah Jones had been invited to a party. It was to be a fancy dress party and on the invitation it said: "Please wear red". Now Sarah fretted because she had no red clothes at all. Then she had an idea. She got out an old blue frock from the back of the cupboard. "I'll dye it red," she thought.

She mixed a big tub of red dye

and was just about to put the dress into it, when along came the invisible imp. "Here's some fun!" he thought. "I'll turn the dye blue. Then she won't know why her dress hasn't changed colour. Won't that be funny!" And he started giggling to himself at the thought of it. He danced up and down on the edge of the tub, thinking up a really evil spell to turn the dye blue. But he laughed so much to himself that he slipped and fell right into the bright red mixture. Fast as lightning out he scrambled and cast his spell.

Sure enough Sarah fished out the dress from the tub, and to her dismay saw that it was exactly the same colour as when she had put it into the dye. She was about to peer into the tub when something caught her eye. For there, sitting on the table, chuckling to himself and holding his sides with laughter, was a bright red imp. And there was a trail of tiny red footprints from the tub of dye to the table. The silly imp had no idea that he was no longer invisible and that Sarah could see him as plain as the nose on her face!

In a flash Sarah realised what had happened. She chased the imp out of the house and down the street and, I'm glad to say, he wasn't able to play his mischievous tricks ever again.

The Magic Tree

TOMMY RUBBED his eyes, blinked hard, and looked out of his bedroom window again. But it was still there — an enormous oak tree that definitely hadn't been there yesterday! If it had been there, he'd have known all about it for sure. For a start he would have climbed up it, for Tommy loved nothing better than climbing trees.

No, this tree was definitely not there yesterday! Tommy sat staring at the tree in wonder and disbelief. The tree stood there, outside his bedroom window, with its huge, spreading branches almost asking to be climbed. Tommy wondered how on earth it had suddenly got there, but he decided that before he wondered about that too much, he had better go and climb it first. After all, there was always time later to wonder about things but never enough time to do things, he thought.

As soon as he was dressed, he ran outside to take a closer look at the new tree. It seemed just like any other big oak tree. It had lots of wide, inviting branches and lots of green, rounded leaves. And it had deep, furrowed bark just like any other oak tree.

Tommy couldn't resist any longer. On to the lowest branch he stepped and then up to the next. The tree seemed so easy to climb. There were branches everywhere. In no time at all, he was in a green, leafy canopy. He couldn't even see the ground any more. But something seemed not quite right. The branches beneath his feet seemed to be so big now that he could stand up on them and walk in any direction. And the branches all around him seemed just like trees themselves. In fact, he suddenly realised that he wasn't any longer climbing a tree, but standing in a whole forest full of trees.

Tommy didn't like this at all, and thought he had better get down. But where was down? All he could see were tall, swaying trees and here and there a twisty path leading off even deeper into the forest. Tommy didn't know how he had done it, but he had somehow got himself completely lost in a forest, and he hadn't even had breakfast yet!

Worse still, it seemed to be

getting dark. "Quick, over here!" a voice suddenly called out. Tommy was very startled, but he was even more startled when he saw that the voice belonged to a squirrel.

"You can speak!" blurted out Tommy.

"Of course I can speak!" snapped the squirrel. "Now listen. You are in great danger, and there's no time to lose if we are to save you from the clutches of the evil Wizard of the Woods."

The squirrel quickly explained that, long ago, a spell had been cast on the forest and it had become enchanted. Every now and again, the Wizard of the Woods, who ruled the forest, lured an unsuspecting person into his realm by making a tree appear. Once you climbed the tree, you entered the forest. Escape was almost impossible.

"But why does the Wizard of the Woods want to lure people into the forest?" asked Tommy, rather hoping that he didn't have to hear the answer.

"To turn them into fertilizer to make the trees grow," said the squirrel.

Tommy didn't really know what fertilizer was, but it sounded rather nasty. He was pleased when the squirrel suddenly said, "There is just one way to get you out of here. But we must hurry. Soon it will be dark and the Wizard of the Woods will awake. Once he awakes, he will smell your blood and he will capture you."

With that, the squirrel jumped up the nearest tree. "Follow me," he said.

Tommy immediately climbed after the squirrel. "Where are we going?" he panted as they climbed higher and higher.

"To the top of the tallest tree in the forest," the squirrel answered as they clambered from tree to tree, climbing ever higher.

"But why?" asked Tommy.

"Because that's the only way to escape. You'll see!" said the squirrel.

Eventually they stopped climbing. They were at the top of the tallest tree in the forest. Below them and around them was nothing but more trees. Tommy looked up, and at last he could see the clear, twilight sky. He also noticed something rather strange. All the leaves at the top of the tallest tree were enormous.

"Quick, time is running out," said the squirrel. "Sit on this leaf and hold tight."

Tommy sat on one of the huge leaves. The squirrel whistled, and before Tommy could blink he had been joined by a hundred more squirrels. They each took hold of the branch to which the leaf was attached. With a great heave, they pulled and pulled until the branch was bent backwards. Suddenly they let go. With a mighty "TWANG", the branch, with Tommy and the leaf attached, sprang forward. As it did so Tommy and the leaf were launched into the air. High above the trees they soared until, ever so slowly, they began to float down to earth. Down, down, they went, until they landed with a bump.

Tommy opened his eyes to find himself on his bedroom floor. He ran over to the window and looked out. The magic tree was nowhere to be seen. It had gone as quickly as it had appeared. But perhaps it had never been there at all. Maybe it was just a dream. What do you think?

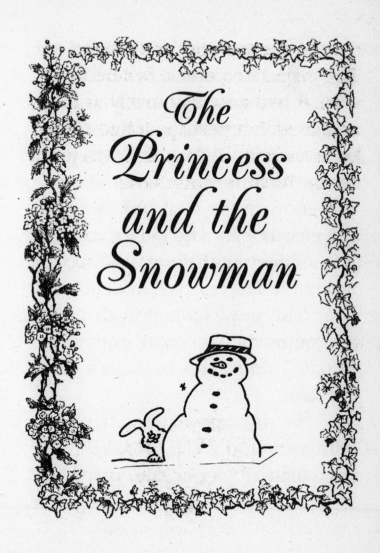

The Princess and the Snowman

ONE MORNING Princess Bella looked out of her bedroom window and saw that the palace was covered in a thick layer of snow. Snow lay on the turrets and along the tops of the walls. There was snow in the well and snow on the guards' hats. The palace garden was so deep with snow it looked as though it was covered in delicious icing. The snow looked fresh, inviting and untouched — apart from a line of paw prints made by Bella's pet cat, Beau.

The princess clapped her hands with glee. "I'm going to make a snowman," she cried, and rushed off to find her warmest coat and gloves.

Soon she was busy in the garden rolling a great ball of snow for the snowman's body and another one for his head.

At last the snowman was finished, and she put an old hat on his head and a scarf around his neck.

"Now," thought Princess Bella, "he needs a face." Turning to Beau she said, "Go and find the snowman a nose."

"Meiow!" said Beau and trotted off. Bella found three lumps of coal and stuck them in a row on the snowman's head to make a mouth. Then she stuck a stone on each side of his head for ears. Beau came back with a piece of carrot in her mouth.

"Well done, Beau," said Bella. "That's perfect for a nose." And she stuck the carrot in place.

At that moment there was a call from a palace window. "Bella, Bella! Come inside at once. It's time for your lessons," called the queen. Bella

ran indoors and, do you know, she forgot all about giving the snowman a pair of eyes.

"I wonder when the princess will come and give me my eyes," thought the snowman wistfully. "I'd better keep my wits about me." He listened hard with his stone ears and sniffed with his carrot nose, but there was no-one there.

Night came and all the lights in the palace went out. In the middle of the night, a storm blew up. The windows of the palace rattled, the trees creaked and groaned and the wind moaned. The snowman strained his stone ears even harder and now he could hear a fearsome icy jangle and a piercing, shrieking laugh. It was the Ice Queen. As she blew past the snowman, he felt the Ice Queen's cold breath on his snowy cheek and the touch of her icicle fingers on his snowy brow. The snowman shivered with fear. Now he heard the Ice Queen's icy tap, tap, tap on the palace door and her howl as she slipped through the keyhole. There was silence for a while, then suddenly the snowman heard a window being flung open and the Ice Queen's cruel laugh.

"She's leaving," thought the snowman with relief.

But what was this? Now he could hear the sound of a girl

sobbing and as the Ice Queen passed he heard Princess Bella's voice calling, "Help me!" Then there was silence again, save for the sound of the wind in the trees.

"She's carried off the princess," thought the snowman. "There's only one thing to do!" He drew his breath and with all his might he shouted through his coal lips, "Heeelp!" He thought to himself, "No-one will hear

my shouts above the noise of the wind."

But soon he felt a warm glow on his cheek. "Can I help?" said a soft, kindly voice. "I am the South Wind and I can see you're in trouble."

The snowman could hardly believe his stone ears. "Oh, yes, please help," he cried. "The Ice Queen has carried off Princess Bella and I'm afraid she may die of cold."

"I'll see what I can do," said the South Wind gently, and she started to blow a warm wind. She blew and she blew and soon the Ice Queen's icy arms began to melt. Then Bella was able to slip from her cold grasp.

"It was the snowman who saved

you," whispered the South Wind in Bella's ear as she carried her back to the palace.

Bella could hear the drip, drip, sound of snow being melted by the South Wind's warm breath. As she reached the palace gate, the sun was rising and the snow in the garden was turning to slush. "I must see my snowman before he is gone," she thought.

There he was on the lawn. His hat was starting to slide off his head and his mouth was all crooked. She rushed over to him and to her astonishment he spoke.

"Please give me my eyes before I melt completely," he begged.

"Yes, of course I will," Bella replied. Quickly she fixed two pieces of coal in place on his melting face.

"You are so lovely," said the snowman, looking at her with his coal eyes. "I have one last request before I'm gone. Will you marry me?"

"Why, I will!" said Bella without thinking twice — for how could she refuse the request of the one who had saved her from the Ice Queen?

Bella could not bear to think that the snowman was melting away. She glanced down so that he would not see that she was crying.

"Bella," he said. She looked up and there standing before her was a prince. For once in her life she was speechless.

"Long ago, the Ice Queen carried me away — just like she did to you. She cast a spell on me that meant I could only return to earth as falling snow. But by agreeing to marry me you have broken the spell," said the prince.

And so Bella and the prince were married, and lived happily ever after.

The Giant Boots

TWINKLETOWN is usually a quiet place. Perhaps it's because it has such a silly name that not very much seems to happen there. The elves who live in Twinkletown generally go about their business without much fuss, and I can't remember the last time there was anything as dramatic as a fire or an

outbreak of sneezles. (In case you don't know, that's an illness only elves suffer from. It makes them giggle and sneeze at the same time, and it's quite difficult to cure.)

So, with Twinkletown being such a quiet place, you can imagine how amazed everyone was when they woke up one morning to find a pair of giant boots standing on the poppleball pitch. (I'll explain poppleball another time.)

Of course, it would be pretty astonishing to find a pair of giant boots anywhere (except on a pair of giant feet), but to find them in Twinkletown really did seem most extraordinary.

Even before breakfast (and elves, as you know, love a big breakfast), several elves had gathered around the boots.

"I've never seen anything like it," said Mugwort, who was a very old elf and had seen most things in his time, although he couldn't always remember what he had seen yesterday.

"They must have arrived in the night," gasped Umpelty, who had a genius for stating the obvious.

"Well done, Einstein," said Twig, one of the cleverer elves in Twinkle-town, which is not renowned for cleverness. "They look to me," he went on, "like giant boots."

"Well, of course they're giant boots," said Mugwort testily. "No one in his right mind would call them tiny boots."

"No," sighed Twig, "that's not what I mean. I mean they look like the kind of boots that might belong to a giant."

A very long silence greeted these words. Everyone was disturbed by the idea of a giant. Suddenly, all minds were filled with questions.

""Where's the giant?" asked Mugwort, looking anxious.

"Are giants friendly?" asked Umpelty, looking worried.

"And more to the point, wherever he is, and however friendly he is, why isn't he wearing his boots?" asked Twig.

Slowly, all three elves spun round on their heels, as if they expected to see that a bootless giant had been sneaking up behind them in his socks. But everything looked exactly as usual — except for the boots.

"We shall have to have a meeting," said Umpelty, who found it very hard to make a decision without other people telling him what to think.

"We certainly shall," said Mugwort, who welcomed any opportunity to listen to the sound of his own voice.

"I suppose so," said Twig, who knew that an elfin meeting could go on for days without coming to any very great conclusion — much like human meetings, in fact.

We have a few moments, while the elves are getting together for their meeting and arguing about which seats to sit in, so I'll tell you about poppleball. It's a very silly game indeed, which only elves would want to play (with the

possible exception of fairies, who are, if anything, sillier than elves). You have to balance a ball on the end of your nose and run backwards towards the goal, which is shaped like a laundry basket and has, for no very good reason that I've ever been able to discover, bananas painted all over it. The idea is not, as you might expect, to throw the ball into the goal, but to jump into it yourself, without dropping the ball from your nose. Unless you are cheating in the worst possible way (and most elves wouldn't dream of cheating), it is almost impossible to score. Games of poppleball invariably end with a score of 0—0, with the result that the league table is one of the most predictable items ever printed in the Elf Gazette.

Right, now the elves are settled in their seats, so we must go back to the meeting.

The first person to speak was the only elf who had ever actually met a giant. His name was Diggle, and he had once travelled a great deal.

"The giant that I met," he said, "was a really nasty piece of work. He hated anyone smaller than himself and often made them into pies. Perhaps some giants are nicer. I don't know. But what I find very strange about this whole business is that the giant I knew would never have dreamed of taking off his boots. He wore them in bed and when he took a bath (which was not very often). Why has our giant taken his boots off?"

Unfortunately, Diggle had to repeat most of his speech because almost everyone stopped listening in horror when he got to the bit about little-person-pies.

When the whole speech had finally been understood, an elf at the back of the room waved a heavy book in the air.

"I've got a dictionary here," called Parsley. "It confirms just what you say. Listen:

'Giant *n.* A very large person with unpleasant eating habits. Wears seven-league boots, which he never removes.' It sounds as though Diggle is right about the abandoned boots. Where is the giant?"

"Just a minute," put in Twig, "are those seven-league boots? They don't look much bigger than four-and-a-half-league boots to me." (And that just goes to show that Twig can sometimes talk just as much nonsense as the next elf, because I happen to know that he doesn't have the faintest idea how far a league is.)

I won't bore you with the next forty-two hours of the meeting. At the end of them, nothing very much had been decided and just as much silliness was being spouted as at the beginning. It was when Twig was trying to raise his four-and-a-half-

league question for the nineteenth
time that a small voice shouted out
from the back of the hall.

"Excuse me! I say, excuse me!"

No one paid any attention at all.
An argument had broken out about
whether seven leagues was longer
than forty-three furlongs, as if that
had anything at all to do with the
subject on hand — or on foot — or,
actually, not on foot!

"Excuse me!" The voice came
again. "Could someone come and
help me with my boots?"

Again, no one paid any attention, but five minutes later, when
there was a lull in the conversation,
Mugwort suddenly asked, "Did

someone mention boots?" And just as everyone was about to raise their eyebrows at the old man's foolishness, because, after all, they had been talking about boots for the past two days, the little voice at the back shouted again, more loudly.

"Yes!" it said. "I left some boots on your field last night and I wondered if half a dozen of you strong young elves could help me move them."

All eyes turned on the stranger, who turned out to be an ordinary looking elf with quite small feet.

To cut a long story short, the elf was a bootmaker. For the purposes of advertising his work, he had made

a pair of giant boots, which he took around with him on a truck. The night before, the truck had broken down, and rather than trying to tow it with the boots on board, the elf had decided to leave them in the field, confident that the local elves would be talking about what to do well into the middle of the week.

"The only trouble is," said the bootmaker elf, "that the truck is getting old and really can't carry more than one boot any more. I don't really need two, so I was wondering if I could leave one of them here with you."

"I'll look after it," called an old woman who had so many children she didn't know what to do, but that is another story, and you probably know it already.

So it was that the most exciting thing to happen in Twinkletown for years turned out to be about as exciting as … well … as the score at the end of a game of poppleball!

The Travelling Tree

ONCE UPON A TIME, there was a very fine tree who lived in a forest. He was perfectly happy there, surrounded by his friends. He imagined that one day the whole forest would be cut down for timber. Then he would be carted off to a new life, and he would be able to see a little bit more of the world.

But when the time came for the forest to be felled, a very strange thing happened. All the trees around our tree were cut down, but he was left. Now, instead of standing in the middle of a forest, he stood on a huge area of open ground.

The tree could not think why

he, of all the forest, had been left,
and to tell you the truth, neither can
I, but that is what happened. At first,
the tree tried to make the best of it.
It was nice to be able to look at the
countryside, instead of seeing
nothing but other trees. But the
novelty of his situation soon wore
off. The tree was bored and lonely.
The land around stretched, flat and
barren, for miles. After being covered
with trees for so long, it was not yet
able to grow other plants. There
were not even any flowers. The tree
felt increasingly unhappy.

But what can a tree do to
improve his situation? He can't hurry
off to complain to the authorities or

find a more interesting place to live. Or can he?

The more the tree thought about it, the more convinced he became that he could move, if he only put his mind to it. Yes, I know, trees don't move. Well, they wave their branches in the wind, but they don't suddenly stroll off down the street, do they? However, our tree was determined. When he made up his mind that he wanted to move, that was it. He put all his energy into doing just that.

One fine spring morning, when anything seemed possible, the tree decided to try to move. He stood up very straight and concentrated as

hard as he could on his roots. He thought and thought and thought, and suddenly, just when he was beginning to give up hope, one of his roots gave a distinct wiggle.

The tree tried again. This time, another root gave a little twitch. This was going to be a much slower process than he had imagined. The tree realised that he was likely to have to spend quite some time doing warming-up exercises before he was ready to wander off across the open plain. But he had made a start. That was the important thing.

Over the next few weeks, the tree practised hard every day. Pretty soon, he could wiggle his roots with hardly a thought. In fact, by wiggling them all at once, he could make himself jiggle about a little on the spot. He wasn't exactly moving, but he wasn't exactly standing still, either. The tree began to feel more cheerful.

It was after several days of wiggling and jiggling that the tree thought he might be ready to try something more ambitious. He dug his front roots into the ground, lifted his back roots as high as he could, and tried to sway forward. The tree had seen people walking, and he was pretty sure he wouldn't be able to manage that. After all, people have two legs, and they sort of sway from one to the other. Trees either have lots of legs (their roots) or one leg (their trunk), depending on which way you think about it.

The tree had decided that the best way to walk would be to rock backwards and forwards, using his roots to alternately push and pull himself over the ground. His first attempt was not very successful, but it did confirm his idea that this was the way to go. He practised harder than ever over the next few weeks.

By the time the tree felt he was really ready to try to move a few paces, it was nearly autumn. The tree was desperate to begin his journey before the winter's ice made it hard to get a grip on the ground. He told himself that he would take his first steps the next day, as soon as it was light, and settled down to have a good night's sleep, so that he would be fresh in the morning.

The morning dawned bright and breezy. The tree stretched up as tall

as he could, braced his trunk, and wobbled forward.

He didn't topple over. He didn't twizzle round. No, he moved about six inches. He was on his way!

Now trees, even very athletic ones, do not move very quickly. Our tree inched his way across the plain incredibly slowly. But it was still quick enough to make a passing rabbit more surprised than he had ever been in his life. And anyone nearby would have been able to see a kind of furrow left behind the tree as he moved.

If you add together enough inches, you make a mile. And if you add together enough miles, you can go anywhere in the world you like. So it was that the tree inched its way over a small rise one day and saw a little town in the distance.

A winding road led to the town, but the tree didn't think he would be any good at walking on a road, so he set off across the fields. Even though the tree moved incredibly slowly, it still caused puzzlement to one or two local people, who were pretty sure they hadn't ever seen a tree in the fields next to the road. But what are you going to say to your friends about that? "Oh, I saw a tree where there's never been a tree before today. Isn't that strange?" I'm afraid it's you that would be thought strange.

Well, day after day, the tree crept closer and closer to the town, until he was towering over the first little cottage.

Unfortunately, the tree had never seen a cottage before. He didn't know that the people inside need to get in and out, or that it is the door that lets them do this. So the tree stood beside the cottage, right in front of the only door.

In the morning, the father of the family got ready to go to work as usual. He put on his coat and opened the door. Clunk! The door opened about two inches before it hit the tree. The man couldn't see anything through the crack in the door, so he peered through the letterbox. Then he ran up to the attic to look out of the little window there to check that he was not going completely mad. No, there was a tree standing in front of the door.

The man had a vague feeling that he'd seen just such a tree at the bottom of the garden a few weeks back. But what was it doing now blocking his door?

Always a resourceful fellow, the man rigged up some flags from the attic window, to attract the attention of passing townsfolk so that they would come to the rescue.

Sure enough, it was not long before quite a group of people had gathered in front of the cottage. As is often the case with such groups, they were much more interested in talking about what had happened and why than they were in rescuing the poor man and his family inside. "But how did it get here?" the trapped family heard someone say more than once.

"Never mind how it got here!" bellowed the man through the letterbox. "Just get us out!"

All day the discussion went on, with the family inside getting more and more aggrieved. At last the leader of the group, who also happened to be the Mayor, leaned round the tree and banged on the only part of the door he could reach.

"I say! Are you in there?" he called loudly.

I'm afraid that the reply of the cottage's owner is not in the least printable, which is not surprising really.

"We've decided what we need to do!" called the Mayor.

"Thank goodness for that!" yelled the man inside. "What?"

"What?"

"I said, what are you going to do? How long will it take?"

"Oh, we'll have to come back tomorrow," called the Mayor. "It is much too late to start now. We've decided we're going to cut the tree down."

"It's taken you all day to decide that?" yelled the man inside. And there was another unprintable bit.

The Mayor looked up. Was it his imagination, or did the tree give a kind of a shudder?

"It's a very fine tree," he called. "The kind that anyone would be glad to have in their garden."

"But not in front of their door!" The man inside was exasperated beyond belief, but he could see that there was no chance of persuading the Mayor to do anything sensible tonight.

"Oh, never mind!" he called. "But

I'll be expecting you first thing in the morning!"

Even as the townsfolk were slowly walking home, still wondering about the amazing tree, the tree itself was thinking hard. Although, in the past, he had been quite happy at the thought of being cut down, now it didn't seem such an attractive idea. He would never be able to walk across the countryside again! That was no fate for a travelling tree.

The tree waited until it was dark, then it stretched up tall and used every ounce of its energy to hurl itself away from the cottage. The tree had become very strong during its journey, and it had not moved at all during the day, so now it was feeling fresh and vigorous. You would have been astonished to see the speed with which the tree swayed across the garden and into the neighbouring field. Of course, the townsfolk would have been even more astonished, for they were still thinking that the tree had been moved by witchcraft or a freak storm.

But the tree had learned its lesson. Letting humans see what it was doing was going to be more trouble than it was worth. You never knew when they were going to have their axes with them, and although the tree could move very quickly for a tree, it could never outpace a human being.

The tree knew it would have to hide. If it could hide by day, then at night it could travel to its heart's content. Hide? I know what you are thinking. How on earth can you hide an enormous tree? You can't just throw a sheet over it and pretend it isn't there.

But the tree had learnt a lot on his travels, and now he did something very clever indeed. He got behind a thick hedge and lay down! Yes, his roots and his trunk had become so supple, he just lay down, out of sight.

So next morning, the tree-chopping party led by the Mayor was a comical sight. And the next night, the tree made good his escape.

I believe he is still on the move somewhere, and you may well have seen him. Keep an eye on the trees in your neighbourhood, and if you see a visiting one, say hello from me!

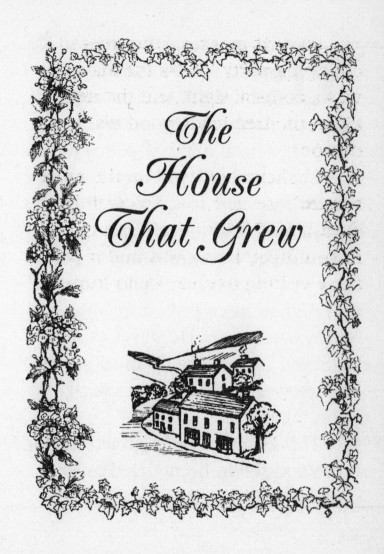

The House That Grew

ANY YEARS AGO, there lived a goblin who was lazy. Goblins are usually very vigorous, hardworking people, but this one, whose name was Boxwood, was really not very energetic. If there was an easy way to do something, he always took it. If there was a corner to be cut, he cut it. And that is perhaps why Boxwood always looked as if he had been pulled through a hedge backwards. He never could be bothered to sew on a button, so his clothes were held together with safety pins.

Things improved a great deal for Boxwood when he married a very sensible goblin called Dahlia. She soon smartened Boxwood up and made his home, which had not really been the kind of place you would want to visit, into a little palace.

Pretty soon, Dahlia's and Boxwood's first baby arrived. It was a little boy, and you have never seen a prouder father than Boxwood. A couple of years later, a little girl was born. Boxwood was beside himself with joy. But when Dahlia had twins the following year, Boxwood's delight was tinged with anxiety. It was all right now, when the children were still quite tiny, but where would they sleep when they were older?

Now, a sensible goblin would

have done as Dahlia suggested and built an extension on to the back of the house. But Boxwood still had moments when he was not a very sensible goblin. He felt sure that there must be an easier way to make home improvements.

A few days later, Boxwood had the glimmering of an idea. He hurried down to the Lending Library to see if he could find some more

information. But he was disappointed. There were lots of books on do-it-yourself but none mentioned what Boxwood had in mind. He knew that he would have to go to an expert.

Old Millet lived by the stream that wound through the goblin town. He was a wise old goblin, with a friendly face. He was said to be wiser and cleverer than any goblin before him. And what was more, he was one of the few goblins who still remembered how to do magic.

There was a time when goblins used magic a great deal, but magic is dangerous stuff in the wrong hands. After some quite awful disasters, it was decided by the Goblin Council that only one goblin in each town or village would be allowed to practise magic, and that would be the wisest, most sensible goblin found to be living there.

Gradually, however, the use of magic almost died out. That was because wise, sensible goblins draw the line at using magic to do homework, brew up a love potion, or paint another goblin's house purple for a joke.

Somehow, the fun had gone out of magic, and it was very little used.

Boxwood arrived at Millet's house early one morning. He was polite and well dressed, so Millet, who didn't get out much any more, didn't realise quite what a silly goblin Boxwood was.

When Millet's visitor explained that he wanted to extend his house because of his growing family, the old goblin thought that sounded an excellent idea.

"But why can't you employ a builder?" he asked, reasonably.

"It's all the dust and dirt and

upheaval," sighed Boxwood. "My dear wife has four little children to look after. I don't think she could cope with building work on top of everything else."

Of course, the real reason was that Boxwood couldn't be bothered to do things properly, but Millet had

recently had his bathroom improved, so he knew exactly what Boxwood was talking about. He could well imagine that anyone would want to avoid unnecessary mess and fuss.

"So you'd like a spell to extend your house?" he asked.

"Yes, please," said Boxwood. "Just one extra room for the children should be enough."

"No problem," said Millet.

He went away into his study. Boxwood could hear muttering and the scratching of a pen. Minutes passed — many, many minutes. Boxwood, who was not a patient goblin at the best of times, began gnawing his knuckles in frustration.

Just when Boxwood thought he would give up the whole idea, Millet reappeared, clutching a piece of parchment.

"Thanks very much," cried Boxwood, seizing it. "Sorry I can't stay longer, but I've got to fly!"

"But…" cried Millet, "I haven't told you how to use the spell. That's most important. You could have a terrible accident."

Silly Boxwood was already halfway down the path. He didn't think he needed any further instructions. It was just a question of saying the spell, wasn't it?

Well, saying a spell is a little like using a recipe in cooking. It may be all right if you just follow the instructions, but quite a lot of common sense is needed as well. And as we know, Boxwood didn't have very much of that!

When Boxwood got home, Dahlia had gone to visit her mother with the children. With the house to himself, there was nothing to stop Boxwood trying out the spell. He looked at it carefully, but it seemed very straightforward. What could possibly go wrong?

Concentrating hard, for he knew it was important to get the words right, Boxwood read out the spell. He turned around twice after the third line and turned back again after the seventh line. Of course, if Boxwood had waited to hear what Millet had to say, he would have known that there is a special way of turning when you are doing a goblin spell. (It's quite complicated, so I won't go into it, but some of your fingers and two of your toes have to be crossed.)

The minute the spell was finished, Boxwood ran to the window to see if there was an extra room at the back of the house. But there was the garden, just as usual. A nasty thought occurred to Boxwood. What if the room had been added to the front of the house by mistake? He remembered that he hadn't actually told

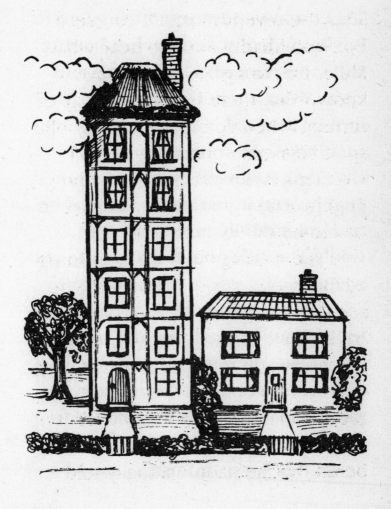

Millet where he wanted the room to be. Boxwood poked his head out of the front door and looked left and right. What a relief! Everything looked as usual.

Boxwood took a closer look at the spell. It obviously hadn't worked. Had he said it just right? Perhaps he had got a diddly mixed up with a tiddly. The silly goblin decided to try again.

But this time, when Boxwood looked out of the front and back of the house, there was no change again. Boxwood felt very disappointed. He had looked forward to surprising Dahlia. He tried again, and again, but it was no use.

When Dahlia walked back down the road that afternoon, she certainly was surprised. What silly Boxwood hadn't realised from inside the house was that the rooms had been added on top. Now Boxwood's house was the tallest in the village, and it quite obviously was not within goblin building regulations, which are not very strict but draw the line at six-storey houses.

Dahlia didn't need to think very hard to guess that Boxwood was responsible. It wasn't very long before that goblin knew exactly what his wife thought of him, too.

"You must go straight back to Millet and ask for the antidote," she said. "All spells can be undone, and this one must be dealt with before the authorities come round. After all, it's not exactly something you could walk past without noticing."

Boxwood didn't like having to go back to Millet and confess he had made a mistake, but he had no

choice. The old goblin was not at all happy when he heard what had happened.

"It's silly young goblins like you who give magic a bad name," he said. "I'm not going to trust you to undo this mess. I shall have to come down to your house myself and sort it out. Goodness me!"

So Millet walked slowly down to Boxwood's house, which turned out to be a blessing in disguise. For there, while he was putting right the six-storey problem, he met Dahlia. She was so obviously the kind of wise, sensible goblin that should be in charge of magic that Millet asked at once if he could pass his secrets on to her. He had been looking for a long time for a young goblin to train before it was too late.

That is why Dahlia is now the most respected person in town. But she keeps her magic books well away from you-know-who!

Toot! Toot!

OLD LADY LOOSESTRIFE of Goblin Hall was a very light sleeper. She often tossed and turned until the early hours of the morning, before she finally drifted off to dreamland. Perhaps it was because she did not get as much sleep as she needed that Lady Loosestrife was always in a terrible temper.

Servants at Goblin Hall changed as often as the sheets. Very few of them could stand the way that Lady Loosestrife shouted at them all day long. She was never satisfied with the way that work was done.

Even when the tables had been polished so that you could see every detail of your face in them, the mistress of Goblin Hall was full of fury.

"I told you to use lavender scented beeswax!" she would yell. "This is lily of the valley, and it smells horrible. Do it again, every inch!"

But no one suffered as much as Lady Loosestrife's chauffeur Buggles. Strangely enough, he had been in her employment longer than any of the other servants at the hall. His father had been chauffeur before him. And before that, his grandfather had driven Lady Loosestrife's father in a very grand carriage.

Lady Loosestrife had never taken driving lessons, and she had not the

first idea about the rules of the road or the workings of a motor vehicle. But that didn't stop her. She regularly told Buggles to change into sixth gear (when he only had five) and instructed him to drive across red traffic lights. But Buggles was perfectly calm. He did what he thought was right and totally ignored Lady Loosestrife, which was just as well, for she could single-handedly have caused more traffic accidents than the rest of the inhabitants of the country put together.

More than anything else, Lady Loosestrife wanted Buggles to hoot his horn at other traffic and at passers-by. In her heart, she felt that she alone should be allowed to use the road, and other drivers and pedestrians should keep out of her way. If she had only known, other drivers and pedestrians did keep out of her way. They didn't want to be shouted at, and although Buggles was a very good and steady driver, who knew when he might be pushed too far and actually follow his mistress's instructions? It was not a risk worth taking.

Nevertheless, some people, of course, did have to use the roads at the same time as her ladyship. They had their livings to earn after all. Then Lady Loosestrife would scream at poor Buggles.

"Hoot at that man! He's wearing horrible trousers. It shouldn't be allowed! Hoot at that driver! How dare he have a purple car like mine? Hoot at that dog! I just know it would bite me if it could. Hoot at that policeman! His uniform buttons aren't fastened properly!"

You see, Lady Loosestrife believed that everybody's business

was her business, and her business
was nobody else's business at all.

Now Buggles very rarely hooted
and tooted at other road users. He
knew it was just as likely to cause
accidents as any of Lady Loosestrife's
other driving instructions. He just
calmly went along at his own pace

and ignored her ladyship. But that seemed to make her even crosser. One day she saw something in a catalogue that she felt would improve her chauffeur's driving enormously. It was a claxon — a kind of hooter-tooter that made an incredibly loud noise.

Next time she went out in her car, Lady Loosestrife popped the claxon into her huge handbag.

As usual, Buggles wasn't doing nearly enough hooting and tooting as far as his passenger was concerned.

"Hoot at that woman in the preposterous hat!" screamed Lady Loosestrife. "It's too ridiculous and

much too much like one of mine.
Hoot at that man with the bicycle!
He looks as if he's about to wobble.
Hoot at that woman with the twins!
She had no business having two
children at once. The very idea! Hoot
at that cow. Hoot! Hoot!"

But Buggles just drove on.
Driven to distraction by his failure to
hoot and toot, Lady Loosestrife
pulled the claxon out of her bag and
opened the window. Oh dear! What
an awful commotion! The preposterous hat blew off in the blast,
hitting the man on the bicycle, who
not only wobbled but fell off, right in
the path of the woman with the
twins, who immediately began to

scream, upsetting the cow and causing her to run straight down the road and through the open window of the fishmonger's shop.

Lady Loosestrife, oblivious to the mayhem she was causing, sailed on in her car, hooting her claxon at every opportunity. In this way, she blazed a trail of destruction through the countryside, and the disasters that occurred in her wake came to the notice of the local constabulary.

"That woman must be stopped," said the Chief Inspector. "I want road blocks at every junction. Poor old Buggles, it isn't his fault, but something has got to be done about Lady L."

The operation that was mounted to stop the claxon-blowing menace was bigger than any ever seen in the county. It didn't take long before Buggles, much to his mistress's disgust, pulled up at a signal from a policeman standing in the middle of the road.

"Don't stop! Don't stop!" yelled her ladyship. "He shouldn't be in the middle of the road. It serves him right if he's run over." And she blew her claxon several times just to show that she meant business.

But Buggles drew to a stop and wound down the window to talk to the officer.

"It's all right, Buggles old son,"

said the policeman. "It's not you we want. I'm afraid we're going to have to arrest Lady Loosebox there, for use of an offensive claxon and causing a breach of the peace."

I will leave you to imagine Lady Loosestrife's fury at:

1. Being taken into custody;
2. Being called Lady Loosebox;
3. Having her claxon confiscated;
4. Finding that Chief Inspectors don't follow orders from members of the public, and
5. Having to wait in a cell with a burglar, a poacher and the poacher's dog.

Lady Loosestrife told the Chief Inspector that she had every intention of buying another claxon as soon as she got home. The Chief Inspector said that as far as he was concerned, she could buy as many claxons as she liked, but she was on no account to use one. He also mentioned the fact that next time she might have to share a cell with a murderer and that no special

arrangements were made in prison for members of the aristocracy.

"What, no servants?" asked Lady Loosestrife, shocked to her very marrow.

"Absolutely no servants," said the Chief Inspector, "and no caviar, champagne or Buggles."

Lady Loosestrife was silent for longer than she had been in many a long year. She agreed to be bound over to keep the peace and went rather quietly back to her car.

"Just a minute, Buggles," said the sergeant at the desk. "I've wanted to ask you something for ages. Just between you and me, how do you stand it?"

Buggles didn't pretend not to know what he meant.

"Oh, that's easy," he said. "After the first year of screaming, my hearing was so bad, I had to have a hearing aid. It has a very efficient volume control

The Imprisoned Princess

LONG AGO there lived a Princess who was good, and kind, and beautiful. She was loved by everyone who knew her.

The Princess was an only child. She would inherit the kingdom after her father the King. Although the whole country was very happy at the thought of so gracious a Queen ruling them in due course, one person schemed and plotted every day to make sure that the day of the Princess's coronation never arrived.

It was the King's sister, Lady Eldred. She also had one child, a pale boy called Ghent. She was determined that he, not the

Princess, would succeed to the royal throne.

Now Lady Eldred had tried for years to show the Princess in a bad light, but she only ever succeeded in making herself look silly. When she was at her wits' end, she decided to call on greater powers than her own. She went to visit the Witch of the Wood, a woman so evil and cold that leaves shrivelled on the trees as she passed. Even Lady Eldred felt a shiver of fear as she approached the witch's lair, but she knew that she had too much to lose to turn back.

At the sound of footsteps on the woodland path, the Witch of the Wood emerged. She cackled horribly and nodded her hideous head at her visitor.

"I know why you have come, my lady," she hissed, "and I am pleased to see you." Little Miss Princess Perfect has long been gnawing at my heart. Such goodness should not be allowed to exist. I will be only too happy to help to extinguish it."

"She will need to be done away with altogether," said Lady Eldred. "She has too high a place in people's

hearts now to be toppled from her throne. What did you have in mind? I will help you all I can."

"No, no, my dear," laughed the witch, "you will *pay* me all you can. I will handle the magic by myself. Although her spirit is too strong for me to take her life, the Princess can still be captured. I will imprison her inside a tree at the heart of the wood. She will stay there for ever. Your boy can become King, and the people will forget all about the sweet-as-sugar Princess."

"That is just what I wish," said Lady Eldred. "I will bring the Princess into the wood tomorrow. You can do your worst then."

The next day was bright and sunny. It was not difficult for Lady Eldred to persuade her niece to walk with her through the lovely shade of the nearby wood. They left the castle together before midday.

When they had wandered for several hours beneath the green boughs, the Princess suggested that they should return home. But they had not yet reached the witch's lair, so Lady Eldred begged her niece to follow just one more woodland path.

"Ahaaah!" cried the Witch of the Wood, leaping across their path. "One of you two ladies must pay with her life for walking in my woodland. Which one is it to be?"

The Princess at once rushed forward to save her aunt. Her kind heart had only one wish — to protect those she loved.

"So," hissed the witch, "you have made your choice."

Her gnarled old fingers flew into the air like bats and hovered over the Princess's head. As the spell was said, the Princess's body changed.

Rough bark grew around it, while the tendrils of her hair became branches and leaves. Soon not even her loving father would have recognised her. Only her spirit, too strong for the witch's power, remained free, throwing a golden glow around the tall and stately tree she had become.

The Lady Eldred returned to the castle in tears.

"I begged her not to stray from the path," she said, "but she would not listen. One moment I could see her. The next she was gone. I searched and searched, but I could not find the Princess."

At once the King sent out all his men to comb the forest for the missing girl. But although they searched every pathway and clearing, and passed several times under the branches of a particularly beautiful tree at the very heart of the wood, they returned to the castle without their master's daughter.

For weeks, the King hoped that his child would be returned to him, happy and well, but as time passed, he had to agree with his people that she had probably been dragged away by a wild animal. He knew that he would probably never see her again.

Meanwhile, something strange was happening in the wood. The Princess's spirit, hovering over her imprisoned body, warmed the trees around it. The whole woodland became so filled with sunshine and warmth that the witch's presence was much easier to spot. Around her lair, the trees shrivelled and died. Wherever she walked through the forest, the moss blackened beneath her feet, and trees shed their leaves as though winter was on its way.

Working in the wood, there was a young woodcutter. He noticed the changes among the trees and realised at once that something evil

was lurking there. But he saw other trees flourish and turn their faces to the light, so he knew that something very valuable had come into the woodland as well.

Then, one day, the woodcutter noticed a tree he had never seen before. It was so beautiful that it took his breath away, and it made him feel at once happy and sad. He longed to stay beside it for ever, and laughed at himself for feeling so strongly about a tree that his work would one day cause him to cut down.

Nevertheless, the woodcutter spent as much time near the tree as he possibly could. One day, as he sat beneath its branches, eating his lunchtime bread and cheese, a little breeze danced through the leaves. It was as though the tree was speaking to him. "*Free me. Free me,*" it breathed. "*Free me. Free me.*"

The woodcutter sprang to his feet. "How?" he cried. "I will do anything, anything at all."

The tree spoke no more, but it came into the woodcutter's mind what he must do. He must cut down the beautiful tree!

For a long time, the young man resisted the idea. He could not bear to destroy something so lovely, but the voice in his head insisted. He knew that he would have no peace until he had carried out the dreadful act.

With tears in his eyes, the woodcutter swung his axe. It sank with a horrible thud into the body of the tree. Tears were streaming down the young man's face as he worked on. Over and over, the silvery blade of his axe swung through the air. At last, with a heartrending shriek, the tree fell to the ground — and a beautiful girl seemed to rise from its ruins. It was the Princess, freed from the witch's spell.

"So much of the witch's magic was holding me in the tree," she explained. "I knew that if the tree was killed, she too would die."

The woodcutter looked around him. The moss that had been black was fresh and green again. The trees that had shrivelled were putting out new shoots and reaching towards the sky.

"I think she is dead," he said, "but how did you survive?"

"I was not thinking of myself," said the Princess gently, "perhaps that is why the witch's death freed me as well. Whatever the reason, I have a very great deal to thank you for."

"Let me take you safely to your home," said the woodcutter, taking the Princess's hand. "There is no need to thank me."

But somewhere along the

woodland path, the Princess realised that she wished never to part from the handsome young man, and he had fallen just as much in love with her.

The King was so overjoyed to see his lost daughter again that he hardly blinked when she told him she was about to marry a woodcutter.

"Splendid!" he said. "It's time there was some new blood in our family tree. Oh, I say, did you hear that? A woodcutter in a family tree! That's rather funny."

Chuckling at his own joke, the King led the happy couple to the Great Hall, where Lady Eldred sat sewing by the fire, dreaming of the crown that would one day sit upon the head of her son.

At the sight of the Princess, Lady Eldred rose to her feet. The colour flooded from her face, and she would have fallen, if the King had not put out a hand to catch her.

"It is a shock, isn't it?" he said. "But such a happy one. How glad you must be to see your lost niece again."

But for the first time in her life, Lady Eldred showed her true colours. All the hatred she had felt for the Princess came tumbling out of her mouth. Even her son was pale with disgust.

So it was that Lady Eldred watched the festivities for the marriage of her niece from the tower in which she had been imprisoned. She felt that the wheel had turned full circle, for as the daughter of a King, she too was an imprisoned Princess.

A Woodland Home

WHEN THISTLEDOWN the elf decided to move out of his parents' home in the trunk of a tree, he knew just what he was looking for. He had always liked the idea of living in a toad-stool house. Some elves these days think that those red and white dwellings are gaudy and not in the best possible taste, but Thistledown thought he would feel like a grown-up elf if he lived in one. The only problem was finding the right property.

Elves do not really have estate agents, but they do have home-finders, who usually know what kinds of houses are available in the local area. Young Thistledown trotted along to see the nearest friendly homefinder straight away.

"What kind of property are you looking for?" asked the plump homefinder, making notes on an official-looking clipboard.

Thistledown explained how much he liked toadstool houses.

"Then I have just the right thing for you!" exclaimed the homefinder. "Come along with me right now, for it will be in great demand."

The homefinder, whose name was Locket, led Thistledown deep into the wood, where some of the trees were old and rotten, while others had fallen and lay across the paths.

"It's not a very fashionable neighbourhood," said the young elf, looking about him.

"It is very competitively priced to take account of that," said Locket severely, "and the price you are prepared to pay is … well … shall we say *modest*?"

Thistledown felt that he had been put firmly in his place, but he was a sensible young elf and kept an open mind about the house he was going to see.

At last, Locket stood still and gestured dramatically.

"Here you are!" he said. "As you

can see, it is part of a terrace of three homes."

Thistledown looked carefully at the very fine toadstools standing at the base of an old tree. He rubbed his eyes and looked again.

"But there are no doors or windows!" he cried.

Locket consulted his clipboard. "As it says here," he said, "these

toadstools are absolutely *ripe* for conversion."

But Thistledown shook his head vigorously.

"No," he said. "I am definitely looking for something that I can move into right away. And I really do think that I should like to live in a better part of the wood. I wouldn't want my visitors to be worried about being attacked by owls when they came to see me. Besides, it's very dark here. I'd like to see the sunshine from time to time. That is essential."

Locket hugged his clipboard to his chest.

"I can see that you are going to

be a very demanding client," he said, "but it's my job to find you what you are looking for. There is another house I'd like you to see. It's not exactly a toadstool, but I think you will find it full of traditional charm."

Thistledown wasn't at all sure what this meant, but it turned out to be the way that Locket described a damp, dark, tree-root house very near to the rejected unconverted toadstools.

"No," said Thistledown. "This isn't what I am looking for at all."

Over the next few days, Locket took Thistledown to see over thirty possible places. All of them, in Thistledown's view, were absolutely dreadful. There was a tree-trunk house that was so ramshackle a great chunk of bark came off in his hand. There was a toadstool house that a family of black beetles had already occupied. Thistledown had a particular horror of black beetles, ever since one of them had crawled into his acorn bed when he was a baby. There was also a disused bird's

nest, which had fallen to the ground, a tiny cave that looked as if it would get flooded whenever it rained, and a little cottage with no roof.

"That is the last property I have to show you," said Locket. "I wonder if you are being quite realistic about your requirements, young man. When it comes to choosing a home, you do sometimes have to compromise."

Thistledown said that he quite understood about compromise, but he really couldn't live in anything he had so far seen.

"I'll know it when I see it," he said of his dream home. "And then I won't hesitate, believe me."

Thistledown's parents were

secretly very happy that their son had not yet found a suitable house. They did not really want him to move out.

"When you have saved up some more, it will be easier," said his father. "It's always hard setting up home for the first time. I remember it well."

"You weren't by yourself," retorted Thistledown's mother. "You were already married to me, and we would never have found our first home if it had been left up to you!" She winked at Thistledown. "You follow your dream, son," she said. "There are plenty of people who will try to persuade you to settle for second best. Don't you listen to them, will you?"

So Thistledown continued to look at possible homes, and he continued to be disappointed. As the weeks passed, he became more and more depressed.

"Perhaps it would be better if you found a home of your own, if this is how you're going to be," said his father unsympathetically, when Thistledown had mooched into the house in a miserable way for the fourth time that week.

"That's exactly the trouble," muttered Thistledown.

The next day, however, he really did try to pull himself together. He decided to take himself off for a long walk, to clear his head and raise his plunging spirits.

In fact, it was a beautiful day. The sun sparkled through the leaves, and little woodland animals were scampering and chattering wherever he looked. It was the kind of day on which it felt good to be an elf, and young Thistledown began to feel better. What was he complaining about? He already had a safe, warm home, where he was welcome to stay as long as he needed. One day, he would find the home of his own that he was dreaming about, and until that day came, things were really not so bad.

Thistledown breathed in the warm, woodland air. He kicked his heels in the clearings and twizzled around the trees. Then, quite suddenly, he saw something that made his heart stand still. It was a perfect toadstool house.

Thistledown stood with his mouth open for a moment. The little house was exactly what he had imagined. It had two little windows and a tiny door. Its roof was red and white, just as toadstool roofs should be.

As Thistledown stood there, staring at the little house, the door opened, and a very pretty elfin girl came out to shake crumbs from a

tablecloth. She saw Thistledown at once and smiled at him.

"Can I help you?" she asked. "Were you looking for someone?"

"Yes, no, yes!" said the young elf.

"Well, which is it?" laughed the girl, folding her tablecloth.

"I was looking for a something, not a someone," said the elf.

"What sort of a something?" The girl looked puzzled.

"A house!" cried Thistledown. "Your house is the most beautiful I have ever seen."

"Well, thank you," said the girl, looking a little pink. "I am very fond of it myself. It was given to me by my favourite aunt, who had to move away. I'm very lucky to own such a lovely home." Then Thistledown found himself telling the girl all about his own quest. She was amazingly easy to talk to, and before long, she had invited Thistledown in to have some dandelion tea.

Over the next few days, the young elf's parents noticed that his step became lighter and his smile came more easily. It was not long before he introduced them to the reason for his happiness and told them that he and his new friend had decided they would like to get married.

So although Thistledown is now living in his dream home, he does not think it's the most important thing in the world. In looking for a something, he *did* find a someone, and that is better than anything.

The Wise Wizard

THERE WAS ONCE a wizard who lived deep in a forest. His life was very lonely. The only people he ever saw were travellers, journeying through the forest on their way to somewhere else.

The wizard looked forward to these meetings. He preferred to live on his own, but it was nice to see a friendly face sometimes. In winter, when the paths were clogged with snow, and travelling was hard, he often did not see a soul for three months together.

One winter's night, when the wind howled around his windows, and a nasty draught was sneaking through the floorboards, the wizard heard an urgent knock on the door.

At first, he ignored it, assuming that it was the branch of a tree or one of the other woodland sounds that come on a windy night. But the hammering came again, and this time there was no doubt about.

The wizard was very surprised. Surely the weather was much too bad for anyone to be out on a night like this?

The wizard went to the door and opened it just a crack, not because he was worried about who might be outside, but to stop the wind howling into his home and blowing his papers from this week to next. But as soon as the wizard had unlatched the door, it was pushed roughly open, and a menacing figure in furs and skins strode into the room, as the icy wind blasted past him and flurries of snow blew up around the open doorway.

By instinct, the wizard pushed the door shut again before he turned to his visitor. He did not feel afraid, but he certainly was wary and careful in what he said.

"My name is Eyebright," he said. "May I have the honour of knowing your name?"

The stranger growled. "It's none of your business," he said. "Give me something to eat."

The wizard looked carefully at the man. He could see that he had lived a rough life that had furrowed his brow and greyed his hair. He looked half dead with cold, and there was a paleness about his skin that made the wizard wonder if he was well.

The wizard also noticed that the visitor carried both a sword and a mighty axe, hanging from his belt. He had no doubt that the man would not hesitate to use them, so he went to his store cupboard and brought out bread and cheese. Then he filled a bowl with soup that had been bubbling on the stove, and put it before the hungry man.

The man ate as if he had not seen food for weeks, as indeed he had not. When he had finished, he lay back in his chair, exhausted,

although the wizard noticed that he kept one hand on his axe handle at all times.

"Have you been travelling long?" asked the wizard.

"None of your business," replied the stranger again. And he promptly fell right off the chair and collapsed on to the floor. His eyes were closed, and his breath came shallowly, as the wizard bent over him.

Eyebright could see that his first guess had been right. It was not simply cold and starvation that ailed the man. Gingerly, the wizard pulled off the sick man's great fur cloak. He gasped when he saw the deep wound in the stranger's shoulder.

Now Eyebright was not the kind of wizard who does spectacular spells or makes himself disappear. He was an everyday sort of wizard, who knew a great deal about wild plants and herbs and the movement of the stars. He had studied for years to learn the secrets of living things and the world around him. As a result, he was a very wise man.

For two months, the wizard looked after the man who had come in from the storm. During that time, the man was hardly ever conscious. In his dreams, he mumbled about battles fought and chances taken. The wizard was not at all sure that he could save the stranger's life.

Very gradually, however, the man improved. His sleep became quieter, and his head tossed less violently upon the pillow. The wound in his shoulder was healing slowly, and the spoonfuls of soup that the wizard had patiently dripped between his lips had given him new strength.

One day, watery sunshine flooded into the wizard's home. Outside his door, he picked the first small bunch of snowdrops and put it in a little pot by the stranger's bed. For the first time, the man opened his eyes and seemed to understand what he could see. As his gaze fell upon the delicate white flowers, his lips trembled into a tiny smile.

But as the man stared around, his fierce manner returned. He scowled and struggled to sit up.

"Where am I, and who are you?" he demanded, staring at the wizard's books and papers.

"I am Eyebright," explained the wizard again. "You came to me two months ago. You were cold and starving, and you had a dreadful wound in your shoulder. I have cared for you as well as I could, and I think that if you are careful, you will now recover."

The stranger was silent for a moment. "Has anyone been here?" he asked. "Who knows I am here?"

"No one," said the wizard. "The weather has been too bad for travellers to venture through the deepest parts of the forest. Now that spring is on its way, we shall see more visitors along the path."

At that, the stranger started up, wincing with pain as he staggered to his feet. He reached for his fur cloak, searching wildly for his sword and axe.

"They are here," said the wizard, holding up the weapons, "but you should not rush off so quickly. You still need rest and time for your shoulder to heal properly. If you go now, I cannot guarantee that all will be well."

With a great howl, the man leapt at the wizard, wrenching the sword and axe from his grasp and hurling him to the floor. Then he dropped to his knees and held the blade of the sword across the wizard's throat.

"If you tell anyone I have been here," he said, "I will come back one dark night and kill you. Or shall I finish you now?"

There was a long moment of silence as the sharp sword blade dug into Eyebright's throat. At first the wizard could hardly breathe, he was so frightened. Then he looked into the angry stranger's eyes and began, very softly, to speak.

"You are a brave man," he said. "From your appearance and the few words I understood you to say while you were ill, I take it that you are a soldier. That is something to be proud of. So, I must ask you, my friend, what are you afraid of?"

For a split second, fury rose in the stranger's eyes, then he released the wizard and pulled himself slowly to his feet. He let his sword drop on the floor and moved painfully over to a chair.

"Your words have pierced my heart," he said. "I am not a soldier, friend, I am a brigand. I make my living by stealing from travellers in the forest. I have killed men, and I have robbed those who could not afford to lose so much as a halfpenny. Oh, I was a soldier once, but I lost one battle after ten years of fighting for my King, and I was punished. After that, my heart became bitter. No one showed kindness to me, and I showed mercy to no one … until I met you. There is a price on my head. Sooner or later someone will kill me for my price, and that is all that I deserve."

The wizard smiled at the stranger. "And do you plan to continue in your old life, when you leave here?" he asked, pouring a drink for the visitor.

"No," said the man, "for my heart is no longer in it. You have reminded me of the way I used to live, trying to do what is right, helping people where I could. I cannot go back to stealing and killing now. But it is too late for me. The next traveller to pass will recognise me for sure, and it will all be over. The King's men will cut me down."

"You are too weak to travel at the moment," said the wizard, "but I feel sure that you could make a new life for yourself in another country. In the meantime, I think I know how we can make sure that no passer-by recognises you."

And that is why, when travellers stopped for a drink and crust of bread at the wizard's door that spring, they found the wizard seemed taller and stronger in his robes, though he was as kindly and welcoming as ever.

In midsummer, the wizard and the brigand parted company. No one would have recognised the clean-shaven man in forest green who strode along the path towards a new life.

The wizard watched him go with a smile. Then he went back to his quiet and sometimes lonely ways. To this day, he is wise enough to see some goodness in everyone he meets, and somehow, that means that there is simply more goodness to go around.

Once upon a time, there was a little elf who lived in a tree. It was a beautiful big house, with a smart door and four little windows at the front. The elf loved her home, but it was rather old. One day storm clouds gathered and a great wind swept through the forest. With a creaking and a crashing, the tree-trunk house tumbled to the ground. Luckily its branches cushioned the fall, and it fell with its windows pointing to the sky, so the little elf was not hurt and managed to climb out of her own front door. But her beloved home was lost for ever.

Now elves live in all kinds of

places. You will find them in toad-stools and among the roots of hedgerows. They may borrow an abandoned bird's nest or make a cosy house in a deserted rabbit's burrow. In fact, they can live almost anywhere. The only place that elves really don't like to live is somewhere that has humans nearby. Elves are always a little bit afraid that humans will try to catch them and keep them captive. Perhaps they are right.

The little elf in this story, whose name was Periwinkle, set to work straight away to find a new place to live. She was very sad to leave her old home, but she really didn't have any choice. She was always a happy, practical little elf, so she made the best of the situation and began her search.

Unfortunately, it wasn't very easy. The storm had happened just as winter was passing into spring, and in springtime, as you know, little creatures are all finding or building homes to have their babies in.

It seemed to poor Periwinkle that every burrow she looked in had a mother rabbit already in residence. And every nest that she thought was abandoned had a bright-eyed little bird making essential repairs before the important egg-laying season.

What about toadstools? I hear you asking. Well, it was a strange thing, but there just didn't seem to *be* many that year. It's like that with living things. Some years there seem to be, say, ladybirds everywhere, and sometimes you can hardly find any.

The nights were still cold in early spring, so Periwinkle really needed somewhere cosy to spend the night. Luckily, she had lots of woodland friends who let her snuggle down on their floors for a night or two, but Periwinkle knew that they too would soon have houses full of little ones, and there would be no room for her. She really did need to find a home of her own.

Then, one afternoon, when Periwinkle was searching on the

very edge of the wood, she came to a wire fence. It was the kind that has great big holes in it, so it was easy for the little elf to climb through. The other side of the fence looked very wild and overgrown, so she didn't think for a moment that it might be part of a human garden.

Periwinkle made her way through the long grass. There were one or two old apple trees, but they looked as though no one was looking after them. There were some brambles and thistles, but they both looked rather prickly for an elf's home.

Suddenly, Periwinkle saw a little house in a tree! It wasn't as nice as

her old home at all, but it made
Periwinkle's eyes light up all the
same. It would be lovely to live in a
tree again!

The trunk was surprisingly easy
to climb, so the little elf quickly
clambered up it and peeped into the
little house.

It looked as though it hadn't
been lived in for a very long time.
There was no furniture and there

were no curtains at the single
window. In fact, the treehouse was
completely empty.

Periwinkle could hardly contain her excitement. It wasn't ideal for an elf, being rather high and draughty, but it was in a tree and it was empty. She would move in straight away!

Over the next few weeks, Periwinkle made the treehouse as comfortable as she could. It wasn't possible to do much about the open door and window, although she did have a word with one or two friendly spiders and asked them to spin their webs across the openings to shut out the whistling wind just a little.

But Periwinkle soon made herself some furniture from acorns and twigs. Before a week had passed, she had a chair, a table and a little bed. The treehouse was beginning to feel like home!

As Periwinkle worked on her new house, spring passed. The weather became warmer and the nights grew lighter. Soon it didn't matter that the wind could blow through the window and door. It was pleasant to have a cool breeze on her face when the sun was at its hottest.

Periwinkle was now so happy in her new home that she never even thought about who had built it. So one summer's evening, she was very, very surprised to hear someone big and heavy climbing up the tree.

Bare as the treehouse was, there
was nowhere for the little elf to hide.
She stared in horror as the face of a
big human boy appeared at the door.
In seconds, his big human body
followed. He seemed to fill the whole
treehouse as he came clumping
across the floor. And then he noticed
Periwinkle.

"Hello!" he said.

Periwinkle wanted to run away,
but the boy was between her and
the door. She wanted to hide, but
there was nowhere to go. Most of all,
she wanted to disappear into thin
air, but although elves are very clever
at a great many things, they can't do
magic like that.

So Periwinkle really didn't have much choice but to talk to the human. He seemed huge, but she realised that he was probably not very old at all, and he did *look* friendly.

"Hello," said Periwinkle in her turn. "How do you do?"

"I'm very well, thank you," said the boy politely. "Are you a fairy?"

"Goodness me, no!" said Periwinkle. "Fairies are quite different. I'm an elf. We don't have wings, you see, and we're much more sensible than fairies."

"Hmm, I always thought fairies were rather silly," said the boy. "It's interesting that you agree with me."

He looked around the tidy treehouse and saw Periwinkle's little chair, table and bed. He even noticed the cobwebs across the window. (I'm afraid he had broken the ones across the door when he came in.) For a human, he really was quite observant, thought Periwinkle.

"Have you been here long?" asked the boy.

"Since early spring," said the little elf. She was feeling much more comfortable now. He didn't look like the kind of boy who was going to put her in a jar and show her to all his friends. The next thing she knew, she was telling him all about her beloved treehouse and the great storm that had destroyed it.

"I remember that night," said the boy. "Our gates were blown right off their hinges."

There was a small silence. Then the boy said, "I'm Jake, by the way. Who are you?"

"Periwinkle," said the little elf. "I'm very pleased to meet you, although I've never spoken to a human before."

"If it comes to that," laughed the boy, "I've never spoken to an elf! This has been quite a day."

Well, the little elf and the boy talked for a long , long time, until they heard his mummy's voice calling from the other end of the garden. "Jake! Jake! Where are you?"

At once, Periwinkle looked frightened out of her wits. "What's the matter?" asked Jake. "It's only my mother. She's quite nice really."

Then Periwinkle explained about how elves are afraid of humans, and the boy looked as if he understood.

"There are things that I'm afraid of too," he said. "And you don't have to worry about me telling anyone about you. I think my friends would laugh, you know. I don't think boys are meant to see elves, any more than elves are meant to talk to boys. You can be a secret."

"And you can be a secret, too," said the little elf. "My elf friends wouldn't like it if they knew I talked to you either."

"Well, I must go now," said Jake. "But I'll come and see you again tomorrow, if that's all right."

"That will be *lovely*," said Periwinkle. "Goodnight, boy!"

"Goodnight, little elf!" laughed Jake. "Goodnight!"

Pumpkin Pie

Written by Angela Holroyd

IT WAS HALLOWEEN, and all the
animals in Catsville County were
looking forward to the annual
Halloween Ball that was to be held
that night. As usual, Tabitha Tatler had
made the pumpkin pie for which
she was justly famous, only this year
she had excelled herself. This time
she had baked the biggest pumpkin
pie that anyone had ever seen. It
looked so tasty that her neighbours
couldn't wait to get their teeth into
it, and it was so gigantic that it had
to be stored in Tabitha's back yard,
protected from the wind and rain by
a tent.

That morning, just after the
wintry sun had peeped out to say

hello, Tabitha bustled along to check the pie. There had been a fierce wind howling around the house the night before and she wanted to make sure that the pie was all right. But Tabitha was in for a shock. Instead of being perfectly round, the pie had a large, gaping hole in one side. And, what's more, it wasn't the wind that had caused it, for all around the hole there were teeth marks. That could only mean one thing — someone had been EATING Tabitha's precious pumpkin pie!

Tabitha Tatler was most upset, and before you could say "whiskers and tails" she had spread the dreadful news throughout Catsville.

The Mayor of the town was furious
— he always cut the first slice of pie
at the start of every Halloween Ball.
It was the grand opening to the
celebrations, and now someone had
actually had the nerve to bite a piece
out of it! All through the day everyone gossiped about who could have
done such a terrible thing — and the
name on most of their lips was
GREEDY GEORGE!

Now Greedy George was a very
large tabby cat with a big, fat tummy
and long, white whiskers. He lived
right next door to Tabitha Tatler, and
the thing he loved most in life was
food. He could eat more ice-cream in
one sitting than any other cat in the

county and, when he was hungry, you could hear his tummy rumble on the other side of town.

About 6 o'clock that evening, George was returning home from skating with his cousins in the country when he came face to face with a group of his neighbours. They were huddled together under a street lamp whispering excitedly. As soon as they saw George coming, they stopped talking and looked the other way.

"Hello!" called out George merrily as he skated up to them. But not one of them answered him. "What time are we all meeting tonight?" George tried again.

"*We* are all meeting at 8 o'clock," answered Perkins hotly. "But I shouldn't bother turning up if I were you."

"I'm surprised you've got the cheek to show your face, you greedy cat," added Tibby angrily.

George was baffled. He had not heard the news about the pie and was astonished when they told him — especially when they accused him of eating the missing piece.

"You needn't look so shocked," said Guss angrily. "After all it was you who pinched the last slice of my birthday cake."

"And my box of chocolate mice!" chipped in Ginger.

"And ever since Tabitha put that pie in the garden you've been drooling over the fence at it," said Max. "Why, only yesterday you said you'd do anything for a big, fat slice covered in cream!"

"But it wasn't me. I didn't steal any of it," George wailed.

But none of the other cats would believe him. After all, he was the greediest animal that they knew.

"And if you know what's good for you, you won't turn up at the Ball tonight!" said Perkins nastily. "You've already had your piece of pumpkin pie — and you won't be getting any more!" And with that they walked off, leaving poor George all alone in the windy street.

Now, George was not a bad cat. In fact, underneath his blustery, sometimes thoughtless ways, he was really quite kindhearted. Why, only the week before he had rescued a tiny mouse who had fallen in the river and had let him move into a hollow log at the bottom of his garden. But, although he was kind, George was greedy. There was nothing he liked better than a plate piled high with food, and everyone knew it!

"They don't want me to go to the Ball," blurted George to Marty Mouse the minute he arrived home.

"They think I stole the piece of pie. It's not fair."

Marty had already heard the rumours. To be truthful, it had even crossed his mind that George might be the culprit. But as he looked at his friend's miserable face, he knew that George was not to blame. He watched anxiously as George sat down heavily in his armchair. Then suddenly there was a loud rumbling noise. It was George's tummy rumbling! George was hungry! He looked up at Marty with a glint in his eye.

"If no one's going to believe that I didn't eat that bloomin' pie," snarled George, "then I might as well eat some of it!" And he rushed out of the door, pulling on his costume as he went.

Poor Marty didn't want to see George in even more trouble. But how could he stop him?

Once outside, George adjusted the wings of his costume. As a finishing touch, he tied a few red and yellow feathers onto the end of his tail. No one would ever recognize him now. He was dressed up as an enormous vulture — a big bird with a huge, sharp beak and fluffy collar.

"I'll show them!" whispered George as he crept along the fence that separated Tabitha's garden from his own. He had decided to creep up on the pie from the bottom of the yard, which backed on to a dense, dark wood. That way he was less likely to be seen.

No sooner had he entered the jungle of twisted branches and scratchy bushes, than the moon disappeared behind the inky clouds. But in the distance he could see a clearing and, in the middle of it, a huge tent — and there, inside the tent, was the biggest pumpkin pie George had ever seen. He licked his lips hungrily at the sight of it.

Not daring to look behind him, he edged his way to the side of the tent. It was quite dark inside except for the glimmering light from a large pumpkin lantern. George was just about to take his first bite from the pie when a ghostly voice behind him said,

"Stop what you are doing! I am the spirit of Halloween...!"

At the sound of the voice, George froze to the spot. He turned his head just as the voice rang out again. It was coming from the pumpkin lantern.

"I have come to give you a warning," it boomed. "I am here to tell you that you are making a terrible mistake. You did not take the first piece of pie, I know. But if you take the second, your friends will be

right to call you Greedy George.
Help me catch the real thief instead,
and you will be a hero!"

Poor George did not know what
to do. The pie looked so tasty, and his
tummy felt so empty — but he
didn't really like his friends thinking
he was a bad cat. So he moved a
little closer to the lantern and
stammered,

"Wh-wh-what do I have to do,
then?" But before the lantern could
answer, a scrabbling, scratching
sound came from a pile of leaves in
the corner of the tent.

"Quick! Hide!" urged the spooky
voice.

George did not need to be told

twice. He dived under the table in a flash. To his amazement, a mean-looking face with glittering eyes popped out of a hole hidden by the leaves. With a twitch of whiskers and a sly look around the tent, a big, brown weasel slunk into view. Standing up on his two back legs, the weasel sniffed the pie and licked his lips.

"Pumpkin pie!" he exclaimed and was just about the take a bite when George grabbed his legs and knocked him off balance. Before you could even say "Jack O'Lantern", the weasel was pinned to the ground. He struggled and snapped, but it was no good — George was much stronger.

Tabitha heard all the noise and came hurrying down the path.

"Here's your thief," said George gruffly, disguising his voice. "I just caught him trying to pinch a piece more pie."

"Well, bless my soul! If it's not Willy Weasel up to his old tricks again," said Tabatha. "I thought he'd

been booted out of Catsville County a long time ago."

"It's off to the kitchen with you," she said, taking the weasel by the ear. "I've lots of pots and pans you can wash up. Then we'll see what Sergeant Sam wants to do with you."

With that, Tabatha marched Willy Weasel off to the kitchen. But when she came back to thank the stranger in the vulture's costume, he had vanished — all that remained was one red and yellow feather, lying on the grass.

George slipped away, glad that Tabitha had not recognized him.

He was not sure that he deserved to be a hero. After all, if it hadn't been for the Halloween spirit, he would have been the one eating the pie. He had not liked the greedy look in Willy Weasel's eye one little bit. And he hated the thought of looking like that himself. Feeling miserable, he was about to slink off home, when Perkins, Guss, and Ginger appeared around the corner.

They had just been trick or treating and their goody bags were full to the brim with sweets and chocolates.

"Happy Halloween!" they cried when they saw George in his vulture's costume.

"Have a chocolate," said Guss, offering up his goody bag.

"Why, thank you!" said George in his gruffest voice, and then he did something very strange. Instead of popping the chocolate straight into his mouth as usual, he put it in his pocket and rushed off in the opposite direction.

"Who was that?" asked Ginger.

"Someone who wasn't very hungry," answered Guss.

"Well whoever it was, it doesn't matter now, because it's time we went off to the town hall to see the pie being cut," said Perkins, "even if Greedy George has been there first!"

Down at the town hall, hundreds of animals were streaming through the large wooden doors.

Everyone in Catsville County had arrived for one of the biggest parties of the year. There were brightly coloured costumes everywhere — witches, wizards, ghosts, and skeletons wherever you looked. The Mayor, dressed as a vampire, stood on a platform. Beside him stood Tabitha Tatler and in front of them was the pumpkin pie, complete with a gaping hole in its side. The Mayor began his speech.

"I would like to announce that tonight a mystery hero caught the Pumpkin Pie Thief, trying to steal a second piece of pie! It was none other than that rascal Willy Weasel, who is now in Sergeant Sam's care."

A loud murmur swept through the crowd as everyone began talking at once.

"Well fancy that!"

"I thought he'd been run out of town long ago."

"What a nerve that fellow has!"

The Mayor held up his hands for silence, then continued.

"We would dearly like to reward the hero, but he has disappeared. All we know is that he was dressed up as a vulture, and he left this behind." He held up the red and yellow feather.

Everyone in the hall turned to look at their neighbour. There were two animals wearing vulture costumes, but neither had the right colour tail feathers.

Perkins, Guss, and the others realized that they had seen the hero on their way to the town hall. They also realized how wrong they had been about George. They had been so sure that he was the thief and now they felt terribly guilty.

"I think we ought to go to George's house and say we are sorry," said Tibby.

"I agree," said Perkins who felt he had been the nastiest of them all. "And we could take our goody bags to share with him."

Meanwhile, George had gone home. He was disappointed at not

going to the Ball, but he was happy about something else. He had given his chocolate to Marty Mouse and it had made him feel much better about himself. George had discovered that thinking about others instead of always thinking about his tummy made him remarkably happy.

George told Marty all about the lantern voice.

"It was really spooky," exclaimed George. "I've never been talked to by a ghost before."

But instead of being impressed, Marty Mouse was laughing. Suddenly, he rolled up a piece of paper and boomed out, "I am the spirit of Halloween..."

"So it was you!" exclaimed George. "Why of all the..." but before he could finish, he burst out laughing too.

"My uncle told me who the real thief was," said Marty. "And I couldn't let you get in even more trouble yourself."

"I'm very glad you didn't," said George gratefully. "Come on let's have our own treats." But when he opened the larder door, it was bare. Then George remembered. He had made a complete pig of himself the night before and eaten every morsel.

"I'm so sorry Marty," he groaned. "It is true that I am greedy. No wonder everyone blamed me for the stolen piece of pie!"

Just then there was a knock at the door and a voice called out, "Trick or treat!"

George opened the door with a heavy heart.

"I'm afraid that I don't have anything for you," he said sadly, staring at his feet.

"It's all right. It's us!" chorused his friends. There was a rustle of paper and they all lifted up a huge goody bag.

"We've come to say that we are sorry for what we said earlier, and to share our treats," said Tibby.

George invited them in and they

started to tell him about the mystery hero. Marty had to stifle a giggle, but George kept a straight face.

"The odd thing is," said Perkins, "that there were two vulture costumes at the Ball, but neither of them had..."

He was about to say "red and yellow feathers", when his eyes nearly popped out of his head. He had just caught sight of George's tail and tied to it were — red and yellow feathers! He had forgotten to take them off.

"It was you!" Perkins cried out at the top of his voice. All the others stared at George's tail as well.

"So you were the mystery hero,"

squealed Tibby excitedly, and she flung her paws around him. "Oh, George I'm so proud of you."

"It was... ahem!... nothing really," said George coughing and turning red. "I couldn't have done it without Marty."

"Nonsense!" snapped Marty. "I couldn't have captured Willy Weasel by myself. You were the real hero."

"You certainly were," said Ginger. "And now you must sit down and eat a hero's feast."

"Well, just a little perhaps," said George wistfully. "And I promise never to be greedy again," he said, passing the goody bag to Marty Mouse first!

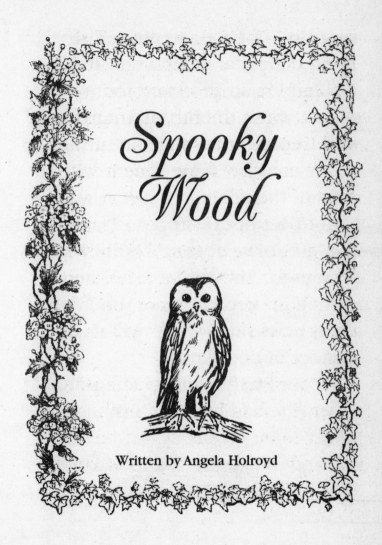

Spooky Wood

Written by Angela Holroyd

IT WAS MR. OWL'S BIRTHDAY. The woodland animals were sitting in Steffy Squirrel's front room talking about the birthday party they were holding that night.

As usual, Maggie Magpie did most of the talking. In fact, it was hard to get her to stop.

"I bet I've got the *best* birthday present for Mr. Owl," she boasted, puffing up her feathers proudly. "It's a real brass ring, which will make a wonderful door knocker."

Poor Steffy Squirrel felt quite upset. She had been so busy

arranging the food for the party that she had completely forgotten about a present.

"I know where there's a lovely present," said Jessie Jay. "It's a beautiful red scarf and would suit Mr. Owl to perfection."

"Where? Tell me where!" said Steffy.

"Draped over a bush in ... in Moleland."

"MOLELAND!" all the animals shrieked out loud. For Moleland was the name that they had given to a spooky area deep in the heart of the wood. None of the animals would go near it — apart from the moles.

"Those bloomin' moles aren't to

be trusted," screeched Maggie Magpie. "If you ask me, the ghosts invited them to live in Spooky Wood, to help them play their nasty tricks on us."

"I've heard they leave messages for the spirits," chipped in Jessie Jay. "Mounds of earth piled high — secret signs that's what they are. Why, the earth itself trembles before a mole appears."

"Stuff and nonsense!" snapped Steffy Squirrel. "I've yet to meet someone who's actually met a ghost!"

"All right! All right Miss Know-it-all!" screamed Maggie Magpie. "If you think you know better than all of us,

why don't you prove it? Go and
fetch the red scarf from Spooky
Wood. If you get back safely then we
might stop believing in ghosts!" With
this she puffed herself up even more
and flew out of the window,
squawking as she left.

"Visit Moleland — if you dare!"

After the other animals had gone,
Steffy sat quietly thinking. The more
she thought about the red scarf, the
more she wanted it for Mr. Owl.

"I'll show them!" she said pulling on her coat and bonnet. Once
out in the wood, she darted along
quickly. But the farther she travelled,
the thicker and darker the wood
became.

The light from the moon cast spooky shadows. What was more, Steffy suddenly realized that she was lost. What a fool she had been not to listen to the others. Just then, a moonbeam lit up a tiny green door at the bottom of a grassy bank. She would never have noticed it had its little brass handle not caught the moonlight.

"Thank goodness!" said Steffy. "I'm sure whoever lives here will help me find my way home." But before she could clamber down the bank, an eerie howling noise filled the wood. "So the stories of ghosts are true," thought Steffy as the earth at her very feet started to move,

rising upward into a huge mound.
Too frightened to move, Steffy
watched in amazement as a small
pink nose appeared from the top of
the mound, followed by a dark furry
head. It wasn't a ghost at all — it
was a mole!

"Goodness me, goodness me!"
said Marmaduke Mole adjusting his
thick glasses. "You look as if you've
just seen a ghost, young squirrel. Did
my noise frighten you?" he said,
shaking the earth from a shiny silver
trumpet. "I always sound a warning
note on this before I surface, just in
case anyone's standing up above.
Wouldn't want to give them a shock
now, would I?"

Steffy Squirrel began to laugh. How silly all the woodland animals had been — making up all those stories about spooks and spirits.

Marmaduke thought it was funny too.

"I have lived here for five years," he said, leading Steffy into his cozy home, "and I've never seen even a wisp of a ghost!"

Marmaduke Mole turned out to be very kind. He sat Steffy down to warm before a blazing log fire and gave her a delicious mug of nut broth.

She told him all about the party and the red scarf, how Maggie Magpie had dared her to venture into Spooky Wood, and what Jessie Jay had said.

"We moles cannot see very well in the daylight," explained Marmaduke. "So we don't often come up above ground. I'm sorry your friends are so frightened of us and our home."

"Well, I'm not," said Steffy smiling. "I will enjoy telling them the truth about Moleland."

"I will take you back to the party along the underground tunnels," said Marmaduke, when they had finished their broth. "There are definitely no ghouls down there!" And with that he wandered off and returned holding a lantern and a blue silk scarf.

"Do you think this would suit Mr. Owl?" he asked. Steffy was delighted. Before they left, Marmaduke collected his silver trumpet and a white sheet.

"I have an idea for these," he whispered mysteriously, but would say no more.

The pair set off along the dimly lit tunnels, with Marmaduke leading the way. Occasionally they met other underground travellers, including a family of beetles scuttling along with their tiny lanterns shining brightly in the darkness.

Steffy was surprised at how many windows and doors there were. She had counted over fifty by the time they reached the clearing where Mr. Owl's birthday party was being held. The tunnel ended at the bottom of a large tree. When Steffy popped out her head, she could see all her friends and neighbours gathered around a big table. The food was spread out and the musicians had arrived. The party was obviously about to begin.

Steffy was about to join them when Marmaduke whispered his secret plan in her ear. Then he put the trumpet to his lips and a loud haunting sound blasted out from the bottom of the tree.

All the woodland animals and birds looked at one another in amazement as a ghostly voice boomed out:

*"Beware the ghoul from Spooky
Wood
From Moleland he has come.
His face is covered with a hood,
He's come to join the fun!"*

With that, Marmaduke loomed out of the tree covered in the white sheet.

"It's a ggg...ghost!" screamed Maggie Magpie. But before she could fly away, Steffy stepped into the clearing.

"That's where you're wrong," Steffy Squirrel said laughing. "This is what you've all been frightened of!" And she pulled off the sheet just as Marmaduke gave another blast on his trumpet. Steffy burst out laughing, and, soon, so did everyone else. Everyone that is, except Maggie Magpie. She was sulking at the top of a tree and refused to come down.

"You need never be frightened of Spooky Wood again," explained Steffy Squirrel as the band struck up a jolly tune. "Marmaduke is the only 'ghost' you're ever likely to find there!"

And so the birthday party began. All the animals made Marmaduke very welcome, especially Mr. Owl, who was thrilled with his birthday present. In fact, it was even better than the brass ring!

The Ghost Train

Written by Andrew Charman

PAGAN PLACE was a tall, dark house that stood on a hill at the edge of town. It could be seen for miles around and all the people of the town were scared of going near it.

Sam's grandmother said that when she was young, an old woman by the name of Mrs Crablook had lived there. She wore long black dresses in the style of a hundred years before, she never went out, and everyone, even the grown-ups, was frightened of her. After the old lady's death, the house had been put up for sale. But no one came to look at it; no one dared to.

Over the years, Pagan Place fell

slowly into a state of decay. The hinges on the doors rusted solid, the brickwork crumbled, and all you could see through the windows was a cloud of cobwebs. The yard was choked with weeds, and the trees had become scraggly and twisted with age. Bats made their home in the roof, and they could be seen circling around the chimneys at dusk. People who were brave enough to pass by the house at night said that they had heard strange noises coming from inside, and some even reported seeing faces at the windows.

When Sam, Billy, and Clara were outside in the street, they were always aware of Pagan Place. In the dark shadows of evening, the house seemed to grow and lean menacingly towards the town.

Billy's grandmother was always telling them that Pagan Place was haunted. But although they thought the house was spooky, not one of them really believed that ghosts lived there. Little did they know!

Inside the gloomy old house, at the end of the darkest passage you could ever imagine, there stood a door. It was shrouded by cobwebs and never opened. Behind it was a room full of old furniture. The curtains hung in tatters at the windows and a thick layer of dust covered every object. Anyone entering this dark and dusty place on a sunny, autumn afternoon would have been surprised to hear the sound of a piano playing faintly somewhere in the stillness.

They would have been even more surprised to see a tall, unhappy-looking man standing in front of the room's gilded mirror. He was dressed in a black suit, with an old-fashioned wing-collar, and huge brown shoes. Taking a deep breath, he pulled his face into a grisly grimace and moaned:

"OOOOoooooohhhhhh!"

"Oh, come on, Herbert," said another man who was lounging on the moth-eaten sofa, dressed as a pirate captain. "You've been dead for fifty years. Surely you can look more scary than that?"

"Well, I'm sorry," replied Herbert in a gloomy voice. "I don't feel well and I'm out of practice. I'm doing my best."

"Look, watch me!" said the other

ghost, and he leapt up, let out a blood-chilling scream and pulled off his head. Then he tucked it under his arm and danced around the room. "See! It's easy!" he laughed.

Just then the ghost who had been playing the piano stepped forward and said in a very wellspoken voice:

"The problem, my dears, is that we don't have anyone to scare. It's all very well pulling faces in front of mirrors. What we need is real, living people to frighten." The others nodded.

Mr Fergusson was well-respected among the other ghosts. He had been dead for over 400 years. He wore very old-fashioned clothes and had once had dinner with William Shakespeare. He turned to Mrs Crablook.

"What do you think, Madam?"

The old lady was busy knitting cobwebs in a dark corner. She made them for the spiders who were too old to make their own.

"I think we need to launch a campaign of terror," she said. "We're wasting our time in this house. No one comes here. We must leave the house and scare the wits out of the people in this town before we all forget how to do it."

With that, the old lady reached over and pulled a rope that hung by her side. The rope fell from the ceiling in a cloud of dust, bringing bits of plaster down with it. Deep in the recesses of the house, a bell rang. A moment later, in floated Clarence the spirit, balancing a tray of tea things on one arm. Clarence was pale and wispy, a shapeless creature who flew everywhere.

"Over here," called Mrs Crab-look. "Yes... er... thank you Clarence."

Clarence flew around the room, his cloud-like body curling around the ornaments and picture frames. The others tried to steady him, but he was out of control again. He floated up to the ceiling, circled three times around the light-fitting, and disappeared.

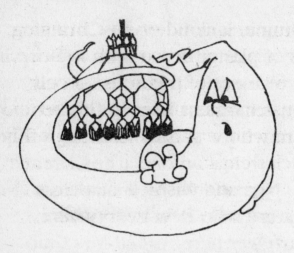

"Oh, dear," sighed Mrs Crablook. "Will someone please catch up with Clarence and fetch the tea things?"

Down at the bottom of the hill, the townspeople were preparing for Halloween, the night when ghosts haunt the living and witches fly through the sky. Everyone was planning to dress up in a Halloween costume. Sam, Billy, and Clara were busy making their outfits and they were all excited. Sam put on his monster mask and crept up behind Clara who was busy finishing off her witch's cloak.

"Grrrrggghh," roared Sam. Clara let out a scream and clutched her heart.

"If you do that once more," she shouted, putting on her tall, black hat and waving her wand at her brother, "I'll turn you into a frog." Sam hopped out of the room laughing and Clara followed, cackling behind him. But they both stopped suddenly in the hall and froze in horror at the sight of a pale, shapeless figure before them...

The spirit turned and raised its arms and moaned. They recognized the voice — it was Billy!

Throughout the town, excitement was growing. Witches cackled and whizzed here and there on broomsticks, monsters clomped and groaned up and down the street, and spectres floated in and out of rooms. The next day was Halloween when there would be a street parade, a giant funfair, and a bonfire party.

The children were planning to be more scary than ever before. Sam, Billy, and Clara tried their disguises out on the family. Their grandmother was not impressed — she'd seen too many ghosts to be frightened of children in costumes. But Uncle Tom was so scared that he let go of his lawn mower which careered straight into the neighbour's pond. Their mother screamed and stepped back into the dog's food bowl, and Mrs Coleman from next door put her hands to her face, ran inside, and wasn't seen until the following Wednesday.

At Pagan Place, preparations were also underway. Mrs Crablook draped cobwebs over her ancient clothes. Herbert practised his menacing faces and Clarence drifted through the eerie house making things go bump. In his room, the Captain pulled off his head and put it back on again several times until the action was quite smooth and unlikely to go wrong.

Meanwhile, Mr Fergusson found some spiders who were happy to live in his beard and busied himself by pressing his clothes. Soon, the ghostly group was ready to give the town the fright of its life. They had no idea that they had chosen to do their spooking on the night of Halloween!

The night started well. A storm raged through the district accompanied by terrible thunder and long, forked fingers of lightning. Owls hooted somewhere in the darkness of the woods and spiders busily wove webs where there had never been webs before. The ghosts of Pagan Place floated noiselessly through the doors and walls of their crumbling home and made for the town.

"I think we should spook this one first," said Mrs Crablook, pointing to one of the nearby houses.

Everyone nodded, and the Captain's head fell off. Herbert stood at the front door and knocked loudly and slowly three times.

Clarence floated up to a bedroom window and peered in, while Mrs Crablook scratched her long fingernails against the downstairs windows.

Inside, the McTavish twins were expecting their friends to arrive at any moment. They were already wearing their Halloween costumes. Bob looked grisly as a green and yellow ghoul with huge boils on his neck. Geraldine wore a wig of rubber snakes that flopped and curled around her forehead.

"That will be the others," said Geraldine when she heard the knock at the door. "Come on, Bob! Let's give them a scare."

The two children flung open the door. Bob roared and dribbled from the corner of his mouth, and Geraldine shook her head and made the snakes wriggle and writhe.

Herbert had never seen anything so frightening, not in life or death.

"H... H... Help!" he stammered, and he turned and fled. He ran past Mrs Crablook who was staring in horror at the monstrous creatures in the doorway. Mr Fergusson and the Captain were already heading for the street, running as fast as they could.

"Quick! Follow Herbert!" they shouted.

The twins were pleased with themselves.

"Wow!" said Bob. "We really scared them!"

"I've never seen Sam and Billy run so fast," laughed Geraldine. "Clara's costume looked great, didn't it?"

As they turned back into the house, Bob and Geraldine met Clarence in the hallway. Clarence floated up to the ceiling and moaned, "OOoooohhh." Then he took one look at Bob, who at that moment was struggling to get out of

his mask, gulped and sped through a wall.

"Bob, that was a real ghost," said Geraldine, excitedly. "It went through the wall!"

But Bob hadn't seen Clarence — he had been too busy trying to free himself from his mask.

"Nonsense," he said. "There's no such thing as a real ghost."

The inhabitants of Pagan Place were a long way from their home by now and in a state of great confusion. They ran down the main street of the town in utter horror. Everywhere they turned they saw ghosts, ghouls, monsters, and witches. At one point, a demon with a forked tail and horns came up to the Captain and shook his hand. The Captain's hand came away at the wrist.

"Brilliant!" cried the demon appreciatively. "How do you do that?" The Captain didn't wait to answer — he picked up his hand and ran.

The ghosts were just passing the entrance to the funfair when Sam, Billy, and Clara appeared out of an alleyway in their Halloween costumes.

"L... L... Look!" stammered Herbert. "More of them." And, without looking where they were going, the ghosts blundered into the fairground to escape.

"Hey, wait for us," shouted Sam after the ghosts, and then turning to the others he said: "Come on, there must be something happening at the funfair. *Be scary!*" So Clara and Billy followed Sam, laughing all the way. Up ahead, Herbert was paler than he'd ever been before, Mrs Crablook had lost most of her cobwebs, and Mr Fergusson, usually so smartly dressed, was looking shabby and red in the face.

"Quick! On the Ghost Train," cried Clarence, spotting a sign. "Perhaps we'll shake them off there." The ghosts passed through the walls of the Ghost Station and climbed on board the waiting train. It was silent inside. Then they heard a clacking sound.

"SSssshhh," said Mr Fergusson. "What's that noise?"

"It's m... m... my teeth," stammered Herbert. "I've never b... b... been on a g... ghost train before. I'm scared." And he took out his teeth and put them in his pocket to stop them chattering. Suddenly, the train gave a lurch, then a jolt, and started rolling forward.

"Hold on everyone," shouted Mr Fergusson.

The Ghost Train gathered speed and disappeared into the darkness of a tunnel. Suddenly, lights flashed and lit up ghoulish faces that leered and grinned out of the shadows. A bright, white skeleton leapt out of nowhere and dangled in front of them. Something wet hit Herbert in his left ear and a mechanical spider fell from the ceiling. The darkness was filled with the sounds of groaning, moaning, creaking, and eerie laughing. Eventually, the train slowed down

and stopped. Mrs Crablook looked at
Mr Fergusson with surprise.

"Well, that wasn't very scary,
was it?" she said.

"Did you see that spectre?"
asked Clarence. "It was rubbish. I
could do better than that any day."

"I wasn't frightened either," said Herbert, opening his eyes for the first time.

Just then the ghosts heard the sound of voices and the train wobbled as people climbed on board.

"Oh, no!" cried Clarence. "It's those monsters again. Whatever shall we do?"

"But look!" cried Mr Fergusson, staring hard at the nearest passenger. "They're not monsters at all. They're children wearing silly costumes — and that has given me a *brilliant* idea!" Quickly, he whispered a plan to the others. They knew exactly what he had in mind.

The Captain unfastened the cardboard skeleton and stood in its place. Mrs Crablook sat in a rocking chair beside the rails and Mr Fergusson stood where the lights would shine directly onto his elegant face.

The children on the Ghost Train had never had a better ride. They whooped and hollered and screamed as the train flashed through the darkness. They were terrified when they saw Mrs Crablook in her rocking chair scowling at them. The Captain horrified everyone by removing his head and spinning it on his finger as if it were a basketball. Clarence followed the train throughout, swooping in and out of the carriages. But the best performance was Herbert's. He stood in the middle of the tracks as the train approached.

All the passengers held their breath and waited for him to step out of the way. But he didn't.

The Captain stepped onto the tracks as well. The train roared straight through him and, as it sped away, he turned and waved at the passengers. When the children arrived back at the platform, they were laughing and cheering.

"That's the best ghost train ever," laughed Sam.

"And you could see right through

that old lady. It was amazing!" said Billy.

"It was as if they were real ghosts," said Clara, excitedly. "Come on, let's go round again."

So they went round again, and again, and again until they were exhausted. The ghosts perfected their act. They had never been so scary, nor had so much fun. So they decided to stay for a little while.

"We can always go home again when it gets boring," suggested Mrs Crablook.

Over the months that followed, the Ghost Train became famous for miles around. Everyday, the carriages were packed with people who wanted to be scared out of their wits. They were never disappointed. People who came again and again were surprised to find that the ride never seemed to be the same twice. The man who ran the Ghost Train kept it open all year round and made so much money that he eventually bought Pagan Place. For some reason it wasn't scary any more.

The ghosts heard about it one day, after a good spooking. But instead of being upset Mrs Crablook smiled at the others and said:

"You know, I don't think I want to go home after all. I'm just getting into the spirit of the thing!"

The Sad Snowman

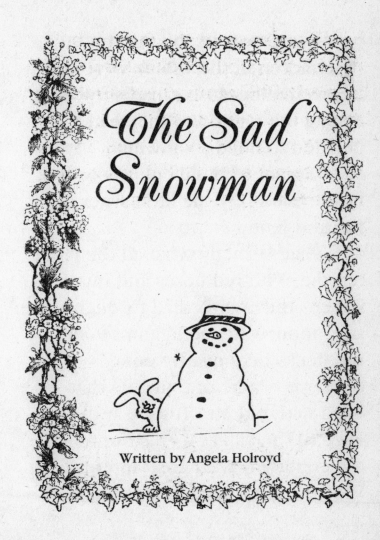

Written by Angela Holroyd

IT WAS CHRISTMAS EVE. All the children in the village were very excited because it had snowed during the night, and they had decided to build a snowman.

"I want to build one as big as a house," said Izzy, the little sister of Jim and Jenny.

That's exactly what all the children did. With red noses and numb fingers, they worked all through the afternoon, watched in amusement by the ducks on a nearby pond. Buckeye — one of four cats that lived with old Mrs. Tumpy at the edge of the village — also watched the goings-on with great interest. What were the children building?

At last, the snow statue was finished. The children cheered loudly when Jim, who was tallest, put the final touches to the snowman's face. He used pieces of coal for the eyes, a carrot for a nose, and put his own hat on top of the snowman's head.

"He almost looks as if he could talk," said Izzy, looking at the snowman over her shoulder as they trudged home for supper.

Soon the snowman stood alone in the twilight. Even the ducks had tucked themselves in for the night. Buckeye had disappeared to find his three friends — Keaki, Hickory, and Kansan — so they too could see the massive snow figure. All four cats gazed up at him in wonder.

"He looks a bit frightening," whispered Keaki to the others. To their amazement they heard a heavy, sad sigh and an icy tear rolled down the snowman's face.

"I don't mean to look fierce," the snowman sniffed. "But it's not something I can do anything about. I'm bound to look this way, because I haven't got a heart."

"How do you know?" asked Hickory, who didn't seem in the least surprised that the snowman could talk.

"Because not one of the children — not even little Izzy — said that

they loved me," said the sad snowman. "And according to snowman
legend, you must be told that you are
loved before you can have a heart.

"You see, when a snowman
melts, the icy water flows into

streams, rivers, and down to the sea if he has a heart — he lives forever as a part of nature. With no heart I will simply melt into nothing. I will just disappear!" And with that another enormous tear rolled down his cheek.

The cats felt very sorry for the snowman.

"What if *we* said we loved you?" asked Kansan who was very kind-hearted.

"That's very nice of you, but I don't think it would work," said the snowman with another sigh. "You see, it has to be said by a child."

For a while there was silence, then Kansan spoke up softly.

"You're not the only one that's sad," she said. "We're all pretty miserable today, too. Mrs. Tumpy is coming out of hospital tomorrow and it's Christmas day..."

"And we haven't got a present for her," chipped in Buckeye.

The snowman thought about this for a moment, then suddenly an idea came to him.

"We must go to the Kingdom of Ice!" he said. "Every year on Christmas Eve Father Christmas stops off there on his way back to the North Pole after delivering all his Christmas presents. He might have a present left over for Mrs. Tumpy."

"But the Kingdom of Ice must

be a long way from here!" exclaimed
Hickory. "Even if Father Christmas
does have a spare present, I can't see
how we are all going to get there?"

The snowman smiled kindly and
winked.

"Tonight is a very special night,"
he said. "On Christmas Eve all kinds
of magic can happen." And with that
he lifted up his large, white arms and
softly breathed a magic message into
the night air.

Buckeye, Hickory, Keaki, and
Kansan all stared hard at the moonlit
sky. One of the clouds seemed to be
floating closer and closer until it
gently came to rest in front of them.
It was a snowcloud sleigh, and it was

being pulled by a reindeer. The sleigh was as soft as a cloud and as white as snow, and within seconds all five of them had climbed on board.

At a word from the snowman the sleigh rose up into the air. And in no time at all the rooftops and trees of the village were far below them. All that surrounded them was the

vast, inky sky and the twinkling of a thousand tiny stars.

Before long, the cats spotted twinkling blue lights in the distance. Gliding closer, they saw that the lights were shining from hundreds of icicle towers which sparkled in the darkness.

As the sleigh glided gently to the ground, snowpeople of all shapes and sizes came to meet them. In the middle stood Jack Frost who led them to the Ice Palace where, seated on a frozen throne, sat the Snowflake Queen.

"Welcome to the Kingdom of Ice," she said in a silvery voice. "How can we help you?"

Hickory explained that they were looking for a present for Mrs. Tumpy and that they hoped Father Christmas might help them. Father Christmas was sent for immediately, but he had just given his very last present away to the Palace cook.

"Tell me what the old woman loves more than anything else in the world," said the Queen.

"That's easy!" piped up Keaki. "She adores trees."

"Then I think I may be able to help you," smiled the Queen. She sent for the Ice Palace gardener and whispered something in his ear. He scurried away and came back very shortly carrying the most beautiful tree the cats had ever seen. It was made entirely of delicate, lacy snowflakes. The Queen handed it to Hickory.

"This tree will bloom through-out the winter," she said, "and will bring your owner health and happiness." Then she turned to the snowman, who was still looking a little sad.

"There seems to be something troubling you Mr. Snowman," she said kindly. "Tell me about it if you will. Maybe I can help you too."

So in a sad voice the snowman told the story of the snowman legend and how, without a heart, he would melt and disappear forever when Spring came. When he had finished his story, the Snowflake

Queen smiled sweetly and took his snowy hand in hers.

"Of course you have a heart," she said. "What you heard is only an old legend. Look what you have done tonight — without a heart you would never have wanted to help your new friends. Only someone with a heart cares for others."

The night sky was beginning to lighten. Soon it would be daylight. It was time for the five visitors to

return to the village. The snowcloud sleigh awaited them outside. Carrying the snowflake tree between them, the four cats climbed aboard. The Queen escorted the snowman, holding in her hand a mysterious parcel. Just as the snowman was about to climb into the sleigh she undid the paper to reveal a large, red, heart-shaped badge.

"This is to remind you that when the thaw comes and the snow melts you have nothing to worry about," she whispered and pinned the heart carefully to his chest.

The next morning all the village children gathered on the green to show each other the presents that

Father Christmas had brought them. It was Izzy who first noticed the snowman.

"Look Jim," she cried excitedly to her brother. "Our snowman has had a present too. I wonder where he got it from?"

"Perhaps it was father Christmas," answered Jim jokingly.

The snowman had to hide a grin. Only Buckeye, Hickory, Keaki and Kanson knew what had really happened.

The Brave Little Bunny

Written by Candy Wallace

BLUEBERRY BUNNY was very unhappy. He lived with his family, in a cosy burrow, deep in the side of Cricklewood Hill. He should have been quite content, but he wasn't.

You see Blueberry Bunny was the smallest rabbit for miles, with the most enormous ears. Worse still one of them always drooped slightly — and because of this none of the other rabbits would play with him. Even his own brothers and sisters felt ashamed of his awkwardness. He felt very lonely, especially now that it was Easter.

All the other rabbits had been excited for days at the thought of

the Easter Egg Hunt. The chocolate eggs that were to be hidden on Easter Sunday had been given to Mrs. Clutterbuck hen at Cricklewood Farm for safe keeping. But now there was uproar at the farm — not only had the special eggs been stolen, but also Mrs. Clutterbuck's four new chicks. Everyone agreed that it had to be the work of naughty Rufus Fox. They were all very upset.

"Can't you do something about it?" one of the young rabbits asked Ragwort. Ragwort was the strongest, biggest rabbit in the neighbourhood. He was also the most unpleasant.

"You have to be joking!" said Ragwort shaking his head. "No one with any sense would pay *him* a visit."

"But someone has to do something," said a small voice. All heads turned and stared at the speaker,

sitting a short distance away. It was
Blueberry. Ragwort burst out
laughing.

"Just listen to that!" he jeered.
"And from someone who's even
frightened of his own shadow!"
Blueberry winced. It was true —
lots of things scared him.

"Blueberry Bunny, Blueberry
Bunny! Whatever he does, he
always looks funny." Ragwort
chanted loudly, and thumped his
paw heavily on the ground.

Blueberry stood up and slunk
off in the direction of Cricklewood
Forest — the noise of laughter
ringing in his ears. Two big tears
plopped onto his whiskers. Blindly

he stumbled into the undergrowth, and flopped down in between the tangled roots of a huge tree.

"It's not fair!" he whimpered, wiping his wet fur.

"I quite agree!" A hooting voice, just above Blueberry's head made him jump. Blueberry looked up and there, on a branch, sat the most miserable owl he had ever seen.

"Shouldn't you be in bed at this time of day?" asked Blueberry, surprised to see a night owl awake.

"That's just it," moaned the owl. "The fact of the matter is — I can't sleep." He flew down on to the ground near Blueberry and held out a wing. "Allow me to introduce myself," he said. "I am Oscar Owl."

"And I am Blueberry Bunny," said Blueberry, shaking the owl's wing.

"How do you do Blueberry," said Oscar. "And what appears to be the problem?"

"*I'm* the problem," said Blueberry mournfully, "just look at me!" Oscar craned his neck forward and stared so hard that Blueberry could feel himself turning red.

"Well..." Oscar began, "... apart from the ears and your small size... apart from that, I can't see what's wrong."

"Isn't that enough?" Blueberry squealed.

"My dear chap!" said Oscar "at least you don't have my awful problem!"

"What's that?" asked Blueberry.

"The fact of the matter is," Oscar whispered, "that I'm not very good at giving advice and helping people."

"But I thought *all* owls could help people. They do in all my story-books," said a puzzled Blueberry.

"That's just it," said Oscar miserably. "Everyone *expects* me to be wise — like storybook owls — and I'm a miserable failure. Why, only this morning, Cock-o-Dandy came to see me about his missing chicks, and I... I simply did not know what to say."

"Perhaps we could think of something together," said Blueberry, who did not like to see Oscar looking so sad. For a long while the pair sat quietly, both thinking hard.

Suddenly, Oscar broke the silence:

"I've got it! I could try to find Rufus Fox's hideout and see if the chicks are there." Blueberry nodded his head. "Then if they *are*, at least we can tell Cock-o-Dandy where to find them." Oscar looked really pleased with himself, but Blueberry shook his head.

"That's not any good. None of the farm birds, not even the great Cock-o-Dandy, would go far into Cricklewood Forest — let alone near that wicked fox. Why even Ragwort is scared of him!"

"I told you I wasn't wise!" said Oscar looking glum again.

"But you are. It's a very good idea of yours to find the hideout. If we *both* went, you could distract Rufus Fox, while I rescue the chicks," said Blueberry, forgetting his usual cowardliness.

"But *how* will you rescue them?"

"I don't know yet, but we'll think of something," said Blueberry.

Just then Blueberry noticed that the sun was going down.

"I'd better be going home now," he said, suddenly feeling scared. "I'll come back early tomorrow."

"Good idea!" said Oscar.

The next morning Blueberry's mother was surprised to see him up and dressed so early. Just as the sun was rising, he set off for Cricklewood Forest.

Oscar was sitting on the same branch as the night before, waiting for him. He yawned widely.

"I've spent most of the night reading *Sammy Squirrel's Riddle Book*," he said sleepily. It struck Blueberry as a very strange way to spend the night, but he didn't want to say so.

"And that's not all," said Oscar, hardly able to contain his excitement. "I've found Rufus Fox's hideout, and what's more Mrs. Clutterbuck's chicks *are* there."

"Did you see them then?" asked Blueberry.

"No, but Rufus was outside very late last night, gathering herbs, and I heard him muttering to himself about how parsley and sage would go very nicely with baby chicken!" Blueberry shuddered. "I think we'd better get going quickly," he said. "Before it's too late!"

Deeper and deeper the pair travelled through the woods. Blueberry didn't like the gloom, or the silence, very much. On and on they went until Blueberry could hardly see where he was going. He kept on tripping over tangled tree roots and crashing into scratchy bushes. It was only the thought of the poor baby chicks that made him determined to carry on.

Eventually the pair halted. To Blueberry's surprise, ahead he could see nothing but dark green pools — murky water surrounded by reeds and plants. Now, the one thing Blueberry was really scared of was water. So you can imagine how he felt when Oscar pointed out Rufus Fox's hideout, sitting on a tiny island surrounded by a big pool. Blueberry groaned.

"Shush!" whispered Oscar, pointing his wing toward the island. There, outside a rickety shack, was the fox lighting a fire beneath an enormous cooking pot.

"But I don't like water," whispered Blueberry.

"Pooh!" said Oscar rather unkindly. "There's nothing to be afraid of!"

"Not for you maybe, you can fly over it."

"Well, you can walk over it," said Oscar. "There are some stepping stones on the other side."

The pair skirted around the island until they were facing the

back of Rufus' shack. And there, sure enough, were the stepping stones, just visible through the reeds.

"But even so..." began Blueberry, who didn't like the look of the slippery stones. "How can I get through the front door of the shack without Rufus seeing me?"

"I've thought of that," said Oscar proudly. "The fact of the matter is, that if you'd been just one teansy-weansy bit bigger then we would have been stuck, but being as small as you are, you can get through that tiny hole at the bottom." Oscar pointed to the back of the shack. The hole was so small Blueberry hadn't noticed it.

"But what if Rufus goes inside when I'm in there?" The thought made Blueberry quiver and quake.

"Don't worry about that. That is where the riddles come in," said Oscar mysteriously. "And when you have rescued the chicks, hide them in this hollow tree and hoot like an owl." He pointed his beak toward a large tree behind them.

Before Blueberry had time to protest any further, or to tell Oscar that he couldn't hoot, his friend had flapped his wings and disappeared.

Rufus Fox was bending over the cooking pot, when Oscar landed on a branch above his head.

"Good morning, Mr. Rufus!" hooted Oscar loudly, making Rufus jump. "And what a beautiful day it is."

"It's a more beautiful day than you think," said Rufus slyly, casting a wicked glance back at his shack,

and wiping his hands on his dunga-rees.

"Yes siree! A very tasty day!" he grinned, showing a row of needle sharp teeth. "But I'm surprised to see you up Mr. Owl — don't your kind usually sleep when the sun's up?"

"The fact of the matter is Mr. Rufus, that I could not sleep. You see, I came across a number of riddles and, for the life of me, I can't work them out. So I thought to myself, 'Who do I know who is clever. Oh yes! I'll go and see Mr. Rufus — he's clever', I thought."

"Well now, you've sure come to the right place," said Rufus, flattered at being thought clever. "I like a good riddle and it will pass the time away until my water is ready." He sat down on a fallen log and grinned his evil grin.

"What shines but is never polished?" asked Oscar.

"That's easy! The sun, of course," Rufus answered quickly.

Better give him a hard one, thought Oscar.

"What is the biggest ant in the world'?"

Rufus had to think hard, but finally he got it.

"A giant."

Oscar looked deliberately blank.

"A GI-ANT — get it?"

Meanwhile, Blueberry was wobbling on the second stepping stone. The next stone seemed a long way off. He dared not think about how deep, or how cold, the water was. Gritting his teeth he took a deep breath and...FLUMPETYJUMP, he landed safely. Just one more to go and he would be on the island. He wobbled a bit more then, holding his breath he leaped forward again. FLUMPETYJUMP, FLUMPETYJUMP! He had made it!

Keeping as low to the ground as possible, he crept toward the back of the shack. Very quietly he squashed himself through the tiny hole. For the first time in his life, he was glad he was so small and that his ears were bendy.

Inside, in the gloom, Blueberry could see a sack by a pile of potatoes — something inside it was wriggling! Quickly he undid the piece of string at the top and lifted out the startled chicks, one by one. They blinked and were about to cheep cheerily when Blueberry held up his paw. "Shush!" He pointed to the tiny ho!e. As fast as he could, he pushed each one through. Then he placed four potatoes in the sack, did up the string and looked around for the stolen eggs. He found them in a bag in the corner, which he had to push hard through the tiny hole. Finally, he squeezed himself through and joined the chicks.

"I'm going to carry you over to that tree," he whispered. "No one must utter even the smallest cheep, or we will all get eaten by the fox!" They all closed their beaks tightly, in fright!

Blueberry bravely carried each chick over, one by one, taking the eggs with him on the first crossing. Once they were in the tree, he opened his mouth and made a very strange sound — a little like a hoot but more like a croak! Nevertheless, Oscar heard it and heaved a great sigh of relief — he was running out of riddles.

"Well, I'll be off now Mr. Rufus," he said as casually as possible, "and thank you for helping me." He couldn't resist adding, "In fact, you have been more help than you realize!"

Rufus headed into his shack and dragged the sack outside. It seemed heavier, but perhaps it was just his memory playing tricks. Meanwhile Oscar had flown straight to the hollow tree.

"Quick! Two of you climb onto my back. I'll be back for you others as soon as I can."

As he soared high above the

tree tops he looked down and hooted:

"Stay hidden!"

Fortunately Rufus Fox didn't hear him, for just at that moment he discovered what was really in his sack and let out a huge, angry roar. Every animal in the forest heard it.

"SOMEONE'S STOLEN MY LUNCH! WAIT 'TIL I GET MY TEETH INTO THEM!" Then it dawned on him. "THAT OWL! THAT STUPID, BLITHERING OWL. HE KEPT ME BUSY WHILE...WHILE..." He was so angry that he could not spit the words out. Roaring loudly, he began leaping around the fire, stamping his feet with rage. He was so furious that he didn't look where he was going and the next minute he hopped RIGHT INTO THE FIRE!

"Yao...ow!" he screeched in pain as he hopped and limped on his sizzling feet over to the water to cool them down.

Blueberry and the chicks heard all the noise and huddled closer together inside the tree waiting for Oscar. Suddenly, they heard a whirr of wings and he was back. The last two chicks scrambled onto his back.

"Hold tight with your claws and beaks!" he warned them as he took off into the sky again.

Blueberry was now alone, but he set off through the trees quite happily. The woods were still dark, but he was no longer afraid. He knew that he wasn't the coward he had once thought he was. After all, hadn't he managed to overcome his fear of water and make the fierce fox look very foolish?

What a sound met Blueberry's ears as he came out of the trees onto Cricklewood Hill. Down below him, all the animals and birds had gathered to welcome him and were cheering at the tops of their voices.

"HOORAY FOR BLUEBERRY! BRAVO BLUEBERRY!"

Cock-o-Dandy had spread the word. Blueberry turned bright red as a crowd of rabbits rushed forward and lifted him onto their shoulders. Mrs. Clutterbuck came toward him beaming and clucking loudly.

"I can never thank you enough! I can never thank you enough!" she huffed and puffed over and over again.

"It was Oscar's plan," said Blueberry. "I couldn't have done it without his wise ideas."

"But my dear friend, the fact of the matter is, that if you hadn't been so small and so very, *very* brave, my plan would never have worked."

"Three cheers for the two heroes," Cock-o-Dandy crowed loudly, and everyone cheered again. Everyone, that is, except for Ragwort. He slunk away, annoyed that he was no longer the centre of attention.

"They'll forget all about him

tomorrow," he consoled himself. But they didn't. The next morning everyone wanted to play with Blueberry and asked him to be the leader of the Easter Egg Hunt. And he was never lonely — or cowardly — again.

In the Doll's House

Written by Angela Holroyd

IT WAS SATURDAY MORNING in the doll's house belonging to Clare and James Johnson. The Johnsons had gone away for the weekend, and the doll's house family was upset because it had lost its cuckoo clock. The day before, Clare and James had had friends over to play — things always got lost when strange children played with the doll's house.

Father doll came into the kitchen, scratching his head, and out of breath. "I have just been all the way to Toy Station to ask them if they have seen Cuckoo," he said.

"And had they?" the twins said together.

He shook his head.

"It's too bad," said Mother doll. "I can't do anything without Cuckoo."

"I was going to bake some cakes, but how can I tell when they are done without Cuckoo telling me exactly how long they have been in the oven?"

"I suppose I will have to put all these packets away again," she sighed.

The twins helped her put the flour, the sugar and the currants back into the cupboard.

"I was going to see how fast I could run around the garden," moaned Ben. "But I can't without

Cuckoo telling me how much time I take."

"And Lucy from Toy Farm said I should go over to play at 2 o'clock, but how will I know when 2 o'clock *is* without Cuckoo?" wailed Becky.

"I blame Clare and James," said Mother doll. "They should know by now that the doll's house is always kept neat and tidy, with everything in its place."

"Clare usually checks," said Becky.

"Yes, she remembered to put the dog in his kennel," said Ben.

"Well, she still forgot about Cuckoo," said Mother doll. "And he's far more important."

"I still think he's somewhere in the house," said Father doll. "So I suggest we search every room."

"But why doesn't he answer when we call him then?" asked Becky.

"Perhaps he does," said Father doll. "But we can't hear him."

"He could be lying hurt somewhere," suggested Ben.

"Oh! don't say things like that,"

whimpered Becky. "Quick, we must all go and search. Come on Ben, we'll try the playroom." Ben and Becky raced up to the playroom. It was their favourite room in the whole of the doll's house. There were shelves with plenty of books to read, a table which they did their colouring, cutting and pasting on, and four boxes of toys which they had not played with for some time.

"Perhaps he's been put in one of those and he's stuck," said Ben looking at the bulging toy boxes.

"Let's search through them." They pulled a box each into the middle of the floor and began to work, pulling the toys out one by one.

"Oh! Look!" squealed Becky with delight. "Here's Mr Clown. I thought I'd lost him." She pulled out a brightly coloured, floppy clown. He had a shiny red nose, a big smile and wore a spotted bow tie.

"Hey! Look what I've found," cried Ben excitedly. He pulled out a lightly crumpled kite, smoothed it out and put it next to the clown.

"It's ages since I flew this," he said.

"That's because the last time you flew it, you let it drop into Toy Farm pond, and then you got it caught up in Mrs Farmer doll's washing and she was very cross," said Becky.

"It wasn't my fault," said Ben. "The wind suddenly dropped."

Ben and Becky continued to search through the two boxes, but Cuckoo was not to be found, so they turned to the next two. Becky found her clockwork train, and Ben found his model aeroplane, but neither found Cuckoo.

"He might have been put in the cupboard," said Becky. This was a cupboard where the bigger toys were kept. They took out the pedal car and the rocking horse and even found their buckets and spades on a shelf at the back, but still there was no sign of Cuckoo.

"Oh dear!" said Becky. "Where can he be?"

"I don't know," said Ben. "But he's not here; we've been through everything."

"So where do we look now?" asked Becky.

Just then Mother doll appeared.

"I've looked through all the other rooms up here," she said.

"We'd better try downstairs then," said Becky.

Becky looked under the cushions

on the sofa. They all looked in the log basket by the fireplace. They looked inside the piano and behind the curtains. They hunted under all of the chairs and under the tables but. . . no Cuckoo!

The cat was the only one not searching — the chair was too comfortable! Mother doll emptied all the sideboard cupboards. She was thrilled to find her favourite, long lost fruit dish hidden behind everything at the back.

"I've looked everywhere for this!" she exclaimed. "We are finding a lot of lost things."

"Yes, but not Cuckoo," said Becky sadly.

They looked under the dining room table and emptied the kitchen shelves. But it was useless.

"I bet those nasty children stole him," wailed Becky.

"Oh, I don't think so," said Mother doll. "Why would they do that?"

"I don't know," cried Becky. By now tears were slipping down her painted cheeks. "All I know is that he's disappeared."

Just then Father doll came in.

"Don't cry Becky," he said. "There is still one place we haven't looked, and I bet those dreadful children played over there too."

"Toy Farm!" they all cried out together.

"Exactly," beamed Father doll.

Ben and Becky walked over to Toy Farm as fast as their stiff little legs would go. Lucy was in the farmyard feeding the chickens.

"Hello Becky," she said "you're early!"

"That's just it," said Ben. "We don't know whether we are late or early, because we can't tell the time anymore."

"Our Cuckoo from the cuckoo clock is missing!" blurted out Becky. "Those terrible children who came to play with Clare and James yesterday obviously put him somewhere."

"Oh! Those two horrors. We've had lots of trouble today trying to find all our animals because of them," said Lucy.

"The cows were in the stables. The horses were in the cowshed. The sheep were in the pigsty and the pigs were in Ma's vegetable patch."

Ben, Becky and Lucy looked all over the farm, even in the tractor shed, but Cuckoo was nowhere to

be seen. Suddenly Ben had a
brilliant idea.

"If those children didn't know
the difference between cows and
horses, I bet they didn't know the
difference between a cuckoo and a
duck," he shrieked, racing off to the
duck pond.

"Why didn't we think of that
before!" chorused Becky and Lucy.
And sure enough there on the edge
of the pond was Cuckoo.

"Cuckoo!" screamed Becky and
Ben together. "We've searched
everywhere for you. Why didn't you
come home?"

"Because I've been enjoying
myself talking to my new friends,"

said Cuckoo. "You've no idea how bored I get stuck in that clock day in and day out — no one seems to even notice me."

"Oh! Cuckoo. You silly bird," cried Becky. "We haven't been able to do anything without you."

"It's true," said Ben. "We all need you very much and if you come home with us now, we promise to let you come back and see the ducks from time to time."

Cuckoo was delighted. He had found new friends and realized that he was important all on the same day. The doll's house dolls were also delighted — now their lives could get back to normal.

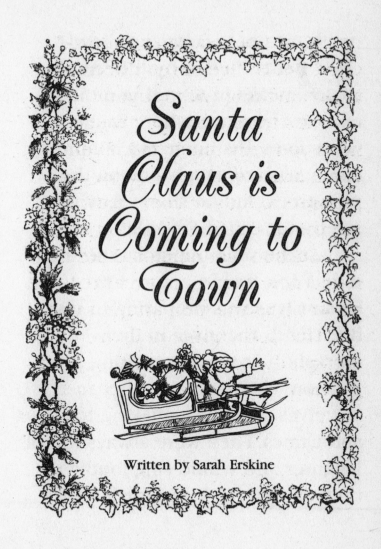

Santa Claus is Coming to Town

Written by Sarah Erskine

D EEP IN a faraway valley, surrounded by the snowy peaks of towering mountains, is the place where Santa Claus lives. His home is a simple log cabin, nestled snugly among the pine trees, and he shares it with a sleepy cat called Fireside.

At the time our story starts, only a few weeks before Christmas, Santa Claus was preparing to visit his friends the elves in their workshop. It was an exciting place to be at Christmas time, because the elves were busy making toys and games. They were always full of laughter and would sing loudly as they dashed back and forth with pieces of wood and pots of paint. Santa Claus liked to go and watch them working and perhaps join in with the singing if he could remember the words.

With a tug that nearly made him topple over, Santa put on his boots. He struggled into his heavy coat, and wrapped a thick scarf around his neck. Then he pulled his

favourite red, woolly hat down over his ears, because it was always his ears that got cold first.

Santa stepped out into the white, crunchy snow, took a deep breath of fresh, mountain air, and began the walk to the workshop. He followed a narrow, winding path between the pine trees and saw the rays of sunlight make the snow glisten. He trod carefully over a small bridge and looked down to see the icy blue water as it tinkled over smooth pebbles. As he walked, he hummed a happy tune and thought about Christmas Eve, for it was the most exciting time of the year for Santa Claus. It was the night of *The Great Delivery of Presents* to all the children who had been good and well-behaved.

In the distance, Santa could see the workshop but he could not hear the elves singing or laughing.

"Perhaps the wind is carrying the sound away," he thought, and he carried on happily humming. But as he drew closer, he *could* hear the elves — instead of laughter, he heard angry shouting!

Santa quickened his pace and threw open the door of the workshop. Inside, a sorry scene met his eyes. Two of the elves, Bright and Chuckles, were standing in the middle of the room, both clutching the same comic book and refusing to give it up.

"Let go of my book!" shouted Chuckles.

"It's not yours!" yelled Bright. "It's mine!"

"Bright! Chuckles!" cried Santa. "Whatever is the matter? Why are you arguing like this?"

"Chuckles took my book," howled Bright.

"I did not!" bellowed Chuckles, angrily.

"But can't you share your things like you usually do?" Santa asked them.

"No!!!" shrieked both the elves at once, and they pulled the book so hard that it ripped right down the middle.

"Now see what has happened," sighed Santa. "Because you were both being selfish, you have spoiled the book for everyone.

"I don't care," pouted Chuckles.

"It was a stupid book anyway," said Bright.

Santa looked unhappily at the workshop. It was usually clean and tidy, but toys and books had been thrown everywhere and he could even see an old sandwich that had been squashed into the carpet. Some of the elves still lounged half-asleep in their beds, while others sat throwing things at each other and being rude. Santa could also see that they had not made any toys or gifts for *The Great Delivery of Presents*.

"Why are you behaving like this?" asked Santa. "The children are going to be so disappointed if there are no presents for them."

The biggest elf, whose name was Sprite, looked up at Santa with a frown.

"We don't care about the children," he said. "None of the

children does as he or she is told, so we don't see why *we* should."

"Oh, dear me!" sighed Santa, and he shook his head sadly. "I know that there are some bad children in the world, but most of them are good. So if *you* are being too naughty to make any toys, then I shall jolly well make them myself! Now I had better go and see how the reindeer are getting on. They will be very sad to hear how naughty you are being."

Santa turned and slowly left the workshop. Behind him he could hear the raised voices of the elves as they began quarrelling and squabbling again.

The wind was cold. It tugged at Santa's clothes as he trudged through the snow to the stables where the reindeer lived. Snow flakes settled on his beard, and instead of looking at the beautiful scenery around him, he stared gloomily at his boots.

Inside the stables it was warm and cozy. Lanterns hung from the ceiling and gave out a golden glow. But Santa looked about and was dismayed to see that all the harnesses, which hung upon the walls, were dirty and unpolished. The silver bells that were used to decorate the sleigh were tarnished and dull instead of bright and shiny.

Even the sleigh itself sat in a dark and dusty corner, covered in cobwebs and bits of straw. It was obvious that the reindeer had done nothing in preparation for *The Great Delivery of Presents*. In fact, they were all sitting or standing in front of the fire doing nothing at all.

"Why aren't you getting ready for Christmas?" Santa asked them anxiously.

One of the reindeer looked sadly at Santa.

"There isn't going to be a delivery this year, Santa," he moaned.

"Don't be silly," laughed Santa.

"I shall make some toys myself and we can still do the delivery.

"Haven't you read the news?" the reindeer grunted, and nodded his head toward a newspaper. Santa picked it up and read the front page. In big black letters the headline read

Santa gasped. The report said that children everywhere were being rude, grumpy, disobedient, selfish, and unkind. Santa could hardly believe it. He slumped into a chair and put his head in his hands.

He could only deliver presents to children who were good. If there were no good children, Santa would be out of a job, and he didn't know how to do anything else. He had once tried to be a plumber, but he caused so many floods that he had to give it up.

Santa sat and thought, shaking his head sadly every now and then. Suddenly he jumped up.

"I'm not going to believe what

it says in the newspapers!" he cried. "I think that there must be some good, kind children in the world."

"You're wasting your time, Santa," sighed another reindeer. "I bet you won't be able to find a single good child anywhere."

"Well, I think I can," said Santa. "It's my job, after all." And he left the stables and crunched back through the snow to his cabin.

Going straight to one of the shelves, he took down a huge roll of paper called *The Great Map of Everywhere*. It was too big to fit on the table, so he spread it out over the floor. Then he held a pin high above his head, and made big circles in the air with it.

Closing his eyes tight, Santa stuck the pin into the map. He opened his eyes to see where it had landed because, wherever it was, that would be the place where he would begin his search for the one good child. He looked down at *The Great Map of Everywhere* and ...

"Oh dear me!" chortled Santa. "The pin has landed in the sea. There won't be any children there. I'll have to try again."

So again Santa closed his eyes, waved the pin in the air and stuck it into the map. This time it had landed in a place called Greenville.

"Then Greenville is where I shall go!" announced Santa loudly, making Fireside jump in surprise. Wasting no time, Santa wrapped an extra scarf around his neck, pulled his hat down over his ears again, and said goodbye to Fireside.

Outside the cabin, Santa tipped back his head and looked at the sky. It was late in the afternoon and beginning to get dark.

"Excuse me!" he called up to a cloud. "Are you going anywhere near Greenville!"

"Why yes," the cloud called back. "I'm on my way there now to deliver some snow. I can take you there, if you like." And the cloud lowered itself down to the ground, sprinkling a flurry of white snow-flakes as it came. Santa climbed aboard and the cloud sailed up and away. They were soon high over the trees and mountains. The stars winked in the dark night sky and, looking down, Santa could see the tiny, twinkling dots of light from the towns and cities below. Santa snuggled deep into the fluffy cloud and soon fell fast asleep. He dreamed of hot chocolate pudding and of trees that grew toffees.

When Santa awoke it was morning, and the cloud had already sprinkled a thick layer of snow over Greenville Town. Stretching and yawning, Santa thanked the cloud for a lovely journey and waved goodbye as it sailed back into the sky. Then he stood and looked around

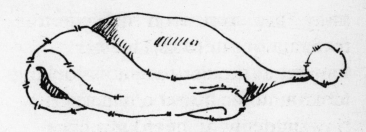

Greenville was a small town with some shops, a park and playground, and streets of snug, snow-covered houses. Santa took a notebook and a short, stubby pencil out of his pocket, and set off to find some nice children so that he could make a list of their names. As he walked, his ears began to feel very cold, and putting his hand up to his head he realized that his hat had gone.

"Oh dear me!" he tutted. "I

must have dropped it somewhere." So Santa began to retrace his footsteps through the snow looking all around for his woolly hat.

Suddenly he heard someone crying. He looked up and saw a girl leaning out of her bedroom window. Her face was angry and red with rage.

"Whatever is the matter?" Santa called up to her. The girl looked down and when she saw Santa she scowled. She did not recognize him without his red, woolly hat.

"I'm not allowed out to play!" she wailed.

"Why not?" asked Santa.

"Because I made a mess of my

bedroom and threw my toys everywhere!" she sobbed.

"Oh well," laughed Santa. "I'm
sure you'll be able to play if you
tidy your room quickly."

"But I don't want to!" she
shouted rudely, and she slammed
the window shut!

"Goodness me!" said Santa. "I
don't think that little girl can go on
my list." And he carried on walking
down the street.

As he was passing a garden he
saw a boy kicking a garbage can
furiously. When Santa asked him
what the matter was he carried on
kicking and spoke in a loud,
grumpy voice.

"I've got to look after my little-sister because my mum's not well and it means I can't play football with the other boys."

"But surely you don't mind if your mother's not well?" Santa was very surprised.

"Little sisters aren't any fun and it's not fair!" the boy complained.

Santa walked on and on, but he could not find his red, woolly hat or any nice children. They were, as the newspaper had said, rude and bad-tempered. His ears were getting colder and colder, so he went into a shop to buy a new hat, but they had completely sold out of red, woolly ones. As Santa left the shop he noticed a big sign outside the Santa's Toyshop. It read,

Santa walked around the playground and then around the park and after a while he sat down on a bench. His ears were very cold, and he rubbed them with his hands to try and warm them. He looked at his notebook, but there were still no names in it. Feeling very cold, hungry, and miserable, Santa decided that the reindeer must have been right. There was not a single good child left.

"I shall have to go home," he thought unhappily, "and start looking for another job." And he rubbed his ears again in an effort to warm them up.

"Excuse me," said a small voice by his side, "but are your ears cold?"

"Yes, they are," said Santa, looking round to see a small boy standing beside him. "Have you seen a red, woolly hat anywhere?"

"No," replied the little boy. "But you can have mine." And promptly he took off his hat and handed it to Santa. Santa tried putting it on, but it was too small.

"My Dad has a hat that he never wears," said the little boy. "Why don't you come to my house for tea and we'll ask if you can borrow it. We're going to have hot chocolate pudding and custard, and mum said that I could bring a friend home if I wanted."

"Chocolate pudding! Why that would be lovely!" cried Santa and his eyes twinkled happily. At last he had found a child who was good and kind-hearted. "I must put you on my list," he said excitedly, introducing himself. The boy said that his name was Evan, and that he was very pleased to meet the real Santa Claus. Then they shook hands and began walking through the snow.

When they arrived at Evan's home, Santa shook hands with Evan's father and gave a deep bow to his mother, and they told Santa that any friend of Evan's was a friend of theirs. They all sat around the fire and Santa's ears got warmer and warmer as he ate the hot

chocolate pudding. Soon Santa had told them all about the elves and the reindeer, and how difficult it was to find any nice children.

"Why don't you take Evan to the workshop to prove that not all children are horrible?" suggested Evan's father. Evan smiled a huge smile.

"Would you like that?" asked Santa.

"I'd love to!" said Evan, and he became so excited that he could hardly sit still. Evan's mother agreed that he could go, and while she made them a flask of hot coffee for the journey, Santa went outside to call another cloud. He looked up,

and there was the same snowcloud
that had given him a ride the night
before.

"I've been looking for you,"
called the cloud. "You left your hat
behind." And sure enough, when
Evan and Santa climbed on to the
cloud, there was the red, woolly
hat. Santa quickly pulled it right
down over his ears and the two of
them laughed about it for the
whole journey.

When Santa and Evan arrived
in the faraway valley, they went
straight to the elves' workshop. It
was even more untidy now and the
elves were still fighting and arguing
with each other. Evan looked at

them all and then he said in a very loud voice:

"Is it fun being so naughty?"

Suddenly, the workshop went very quiet. The elves stopped what they were doing and looked at Evan in stunned silence.

"Of course it's fun!" snapped Bright, angrily. "We don't have to do what we're told, we can make a mess, we can even stay up all night if we want to. We can all do exactly what we want." Bright scowled at the other elves to make sure that they agreed. Then, in the quiet, there suddenly came the sound of sobbing. It was coming from the top of one of the bunk beds.

"I... I... I don't think it's fun," said a small, wobbly voice, and the pink, tear-stained face of Tot, the smallest elf, appeared from underneath the bedclothes. "We don't play nice games anymore, because nobody plays fair," he gulped. "And I miss making toys for all the children. And the reindeer aren't friends with us. And Santa doesn't like us any more. And I don't want to stay up all night because I get too tired. And nobody laughs ... and ... and nobody hugs me any more." With that, poor little Tot burst into tears again and burrowed his face into his pillow. And then, one by one, all the other elves burst into tears as well.

"We're sorry, Tot," wailed Chuckles. "We didn't mean to make you unhappy. And you're right, being bad isn't that much fun after all."

All the elves gave Tot a hug. And then they hugged Santa, and then Evan, and then they hugged each other and Chuckles even tried hugging himself, but he fell over and started laughing. Soon, all the other elves were laughing too and

they began straight away to tidy the workshop.

"We want to make lots of lovely presents for Christmas now," said Chuckles, "but who will you give them to, Santa? Evan is the only nice child you managed to find."

"Don't you worry. There must be lots of other good children," laughed Santa. "I shall find them." So Chuckles ran to tell the reindeer that Christmas was going ahead as usual and everyone began working furiously to get ready for *The Great Delivery of Presents.*

Evan caught a fast cloud back to Greenville and told all his friends

about Tot and the other elves. The
children felt guilty about having
been so badly behaved and they
also realized that it was more fun to

be good because people liked them more. Gradually the news spread and children everywhere started being good and kind and feeling a lot better for it.

Santa flew over the towns and cities, and soon he had enough names to fill a hundred notebooks.

Meanwhile, the reindeer cleaned and scrubbed and brushed. The sleigh was given a new coat of paint and they polished the harnesses until they shone. The silver bells sparkled like diamonds and tinkled a merry tune.

In the workshop, the elves were busy sawing, hammering, painting, and wrapping. In one

corner there was a pile of presents
that grew bigger and bigger with
each passing hour. Every one of
them worked as hard as they could,
and by Christmas Eve everything
was ready. The elves gathered
outside to wave and cheer the
sleigh goodbye as Santa left to start
The Great Delivery.

The reindeer pranced and

danced through the sky, pulling Santa and all the presents behind them. And at the very back of the sleigh was an extra special present for a little boy called Evan who had made them all realize that being good and kind was much more fun than being horrid!

The Christmas Kitten

Written by Andrew Charman

IT WAS CHRISTMAS EVE and everyone in the animal shelter was having fun. They were glad to be inside in the warm and not outside in the cold city streets, fighting over scraps of food. It was bright and noisy in the shelter and full to overflowing with cats of all shapes and sizes. Some were neatly groomed and others were shabby, but mostly they were cats from the streets who had nowhere else to go.

Ginger, the biggest and bossiest of the cats, had organized a game of tag. Cats were running and jumping everywhere. Suddenly, one cat pushed another as he ran past. The other cat pushed back, and a fight started. Soon others joined in. They fell into a heap, claws flashing, hissing, scratching, and biting. Like a hurricane, the fight swept across the room, gathering everyone in its path.

In the corner was a little kitten who was trying not to be noticed. The fight engulfed him. A paw struck him in the face. The kitten heard a buzzing noise and the room spun. Then suddenly he felt as if he was flying. He just had time to see the other cats below him looking up in wonder before he hit the ground with a bump. Ginger had pulled him out by his tail.

"You're going to have to keep

your wits about you if you're going to survive in this place," laughed Ginger. "What's your name, little one?"

"Oliver," replied the kitten, trembling.

"It's a tough life in the shelter, Oliver," said Ginger. "I can see that I'm going to have to give you a few

tips on self-defence. Now, what do you do if a cat comes up behind you without warning?"

"Run?" suggested Oliver.

"No, you spin and slash," laughed Ginger. "Don't give them time to think." Ginger suddenly spun around and lashed out with his paws. His gleaming claws sank into the wall, leaving a row of deep scratches. "That's the way," he said, proudly.

"But I thought cats were supposed to live with families," said Oliver, surprised. "They sleep in front of the fire and lap up bowls of milk and have plenty of time for grooming."

"You're in the wrong place if that's what you want," laughed Ginger. "Around here we turn kittens into street-fighting tigers." And with that the big cat strolled off, muttering to himself.

Oliver washed his paw thoughtfully, and wondered at what Ginger had said. He had only been in the shelter for a couple of weeks and he couldn't remember very much about where he'd been before that. But he guessed he must have been with a "family," whatever that was, and that was how he knew about them. He certainly didn't like the idea of becoming a street-fighting tiger.

"Perhaps I am in the wrong place, then," thought Oliver to himself. Small and weak though he was, Oliver was strong in his mind. He knew what he wanted. He wanted to be in a family, and he was going to find one. He decided to escape.

Later, when the food arrived, Oliver saw his chance. As the others crowded around the bowls of food, he crept quietly out of the partly-opened door. He scampered quickly down the bright corridor and through another door. He was inside a cupboard. Then, just when he thought he'd have to go back and find another way out, he saw it.

A hole. What luck! It was just large enough for Oliver to squeeze through.

In no time at all, he was running along a narrow tunnel. He could feel a draught of cold air whistling through his whiskers. The outside couldn't be far.

Oliver heard voices ahead and suddenly the tunnel opened out into a large underground cave. He could see movement below him. As his eyes became accustomed to the dim light, Oliver saw hundreds of small, furry animals. They had sleek gray fur, long pink tails, and twitching whiskers. They were mice!

"Can we begin?" said a large mouse who had climbed onto an empty can in the centre of the throng. "I have called the family together to discuss an important issue." Oliver's ears pricked up at the sound of the word "family".

"Now as you all know," the big mouse went on, "tomorrow is Christmas Day and we have planned our

usual family celebration..." But he didn't get a chance to continue for Oliver could not hold himself back any longer. He jumped down from the ledge, shouting eagerly:

"Can I join your family? Oh, please let me join."

Chaos immediately broke out all around him. Mice fled in every direction. Oliver heard shouts of "Quick, cats!" and "Run for your whiskers!" as the mice climbed over each other to get away. Seconds later, the underground cave was empty. Poor Oliver couldn't understand it.

"Whatever did I say!" he thought to himself. "Anyway, that's obviously not the right kind of family for me." So he shrugged his shoulders and walked on.

Soon Oliver reached the open air. An icy wind was blowing through the streets, and it had started to snow. Large flakes fell onto his fur and melted. Before long he was wet and bedraggled. The city looked strange and fright-

ening. Lights flashed and cars roared past. Oliver trudged along the sidewalk, feeling unhappier than he had ever felt.

Then Oliver heard an unfamiliar sound. He'd never heard it before, but he knew just what it was all the same.

"WOOF!" it went again. He turned and there it was, a little way

off, but getting closer — ears flapping, mouth dribbling, huge wet paws slapping against the ground. A dog! An enormous, hairy dog was bounding toward him.

One of the cats at the shelter had once told Oliver that dogs were harmless and that they just wanted to play. But Oliver wasn't about to stay and discover if that was true.

Oliver took one look at the dog's wet, wobbling mouth, and fled. For an instant, he was running on the spot, slipping on the icy ground. Then he shot forward, running as fast as he could.

Oliver rounded a corner and

glanced behind him. The dog was getting closer. Just then, a taxi stopped ahead of him. A woman who had been standing beside the road opened the door. Oliver didn't have time to think. He jumped straight into the open taxi and dived under a seat. The door slammed shut.

The dog skidded, spun around twice before stopping, and barked as he watched the taxi drive away through the snow. Oliver crouched under the seat and listened to his heart beating.

"Phew!" he thought. "That was close."

Oliver lay very still. Neither the driver nor the passenger had seen

him. They were busy talking about Christmas Day, just like the mice.

"I promised her one for Christmas," the woman was saying. "But all they had at the pet shop were rabbits and guinea pigs..."

No, they definitely hadn't seen him. The air in the taxi was warm and the vibration of the engine soothing. Soon Oliver was fast asleep.

He awoke just in time to see the woman opening the door. Out he jumped, scurrying quickly away into the bushes at the side of the road.

Oliver looked around him. He was on the edge of a wood. Tall trees stretched up toward the sun, their branches weighed down with the snow that had fallen only an hour before. It didn't look like the sort of place where you might find a family, but Oliver set off to search for one anyway. He struggled with difficulty through the thick snow. Sometimes he sank completely in drifts that came over his ears. Eventually, he came to a hillock which, for some reason wasn't covered with snow. He scrambled to the top to see where he was. Suddenly, the hillock moved. It rose from the ground, swayed slightly, and yawned.

The hillock wasn't a hillock at

all — it was a huge brown bear and
Oliver was standing on it!

"I'm terribly sorry," said Oliver,
nervously. "I thought you were a
hill. I'll get down now and I won't
bother you again."

"Oh, don't mind me," said the
bear, yawning. "I didn't even notice
you. I must have fallen asleep."

"Well, thank you," said Oliver

climbing down carefully. "Actually, I came out here to look for a family, but now I think I'm lost."

"Well, you're not lost now. I've found you," said the bear, kindly. "But I don't know where you'll find a family around here. You can come and meet my family if you like. We're just getting ready for Christmas."

Oliver said he would love to meet a bear family so the two animals walked on together through the sunshine. Soon they came to a big cave in the side of a hill.

"This is where we live," said the bear. "You're lucky to find us up. We usually sleep at this time of the year because of the cold."

Then the bear introduced Oliver to his mother and father and all his brothers and sisters, and they all sat down for something to eat. There were berries and grasses, funny-looking grubs, and bowls of honey, but no saucers of milk. Oliver decided that he wasn't very hungry.

After the meal, the bears rolled in the snow to clean their fur and started yawning noisily.

"Time for bed, I think," said the first bear. "Are you coming, little animal?"

But Oliver had decided that a bear family was not the right sort of family for him. It appeared that they did not have fires or bowls of milk, and he really didn't like the idea of rolling in the snow to get clean. So he thanked them for their kindness and told them politely that he would continue on his way.

The bears waved Oliver goodbye and he promised that he would return to visit them in the spring when they would all be feeling more lively.

The sun was hanging low in the sky as Oliver set off once more through the trees. Every now and then, a tree would shiver in the wind and send a cascade of flakes to the ground.

Everywhere Oliver looked he

could see footprints in the snow. Oliver tried to follow them, but he wasn't sure in which direction they were going. He went around in circles several times before reaching the other side of the woods.

Listening hard, Oliver could hear unfamiliar noises — animal noises that he had not heard before. He climbed a tall bank and peered cautiously over.

On the other side was the biggest animal Oliver had ever seen. It had huge sturdy legs that looked like tree trunks, large flapping ears, and an impossibly long nose. The strange animal was eating bundles of hay.

"Hello," said Oliver, bravely.

"And how are you this fine festive season?" said the animal in an important voice. "Would you like some supper? I have an apple here somewhere that I was saving for just such a visit."

The animal stepped back to rummage in the hay. There was a loud crunch.

"Oh, bother," said the animal, lifting its foot from the squashed apple.

"Actually, I wasn't looking for food," said Oliver. "I am looking for a family. Do you know where I can find one?"

"Well, we all belong to the same family really," replied the animal thoughtfully. "Each and every one of us belongs to the family of animals."

"Of course, we're not all the same," the animal continued. "Some of us are mammals, and others are reptiles or birds. Were you looking for any particular species? We've got most of them here. Take me for instance. I'm an Indian elephant. That's Mammalia, Proboscidea, *Elephas maximus*. What are you?"

"I'm a kitten," replied Oliver who was very confused and wished that he had a more important-sounding name.

"Come over here and let me have a closer look," said the elephant. "Yes, I see — four paws, fur, whiskers, long tail. Can you see in the dark?"

"Oh, yes," replied Oliver. "Very well!"

"In that case there can be no doubt about it," said the elephant. "You are a cat, a carnivore of the family Felidae. *Felis catus* to be precise. I would suggest that you continue your search for a family in the cat's enclosure. It's at the far end of the zoo."

Oliver thanked the elephant and hurried away. When he looked back at the huge animal, it was studying the squashed apple.

"Yes" Oliver heard the elephant say to itself. "Difficult things, flat apples. Now if I can just get my trunk underneath it, perhaps. . ."

Oliver scampered off through the zoo. He passed many strange and wonderful animals that he had never seen before. The chimps were throwing snowballs at each other. An owl winked a large, orange eye at him. Snakes curled around branches and flicked out their tongues as he passed. A giraffe peered down at him from a great height. He never realised that there were so many animal families to choose from.

Eventually, Oliver arrived at the cat's enclosure. He could hear a

fierce growling coming from inside.
But he went bravely up to the
fence and peeped in all the same.
Inside was a huge cat with a long,
sleek body striped with orange,
white, and black.

"Excuse me," said Oliver.

The cat turned slowly and
looked at him. Then it padded
silently towards him and stared
unblinkingly through the fence.

"I'm a cat," said Oliver, trying
not to be put off by the other cat's
menacing look. "And I'd like to join
your family. Can I come and live
with you?"

The huge cat looked at Oliver
and slowly raised its eyebrows.

"Can you come and live with *ME?*" it repeated.

"Do you know *who I am?*" Oliver had to admit that he hadn't the faintest idea.

"I am a tiger," said the tiger. "I am the biggest and fiercest cat in the whole world. I am royalty, I am."

There was a pause while the tiger looked Oliver up and down again, and then he growled:

"SCRAM, PUSSYCAT!"

"So that's what a tiger looks like," thought Oliver, remembering his conversation with Ginger. "Well, I never wanted to be one of them anyway."

He went up to the next cage

and peered in nervously. Inside there was another huge cat, this time with a long, shaggy mane.

"Good evening," said Oliver politely. "Do you have a family I could join?" But to Oliver's dismay the big cat just laughed.

"Ha, ha, ha!" he snarled. "I am a lion, King of all the Cats. You're far too small and scrawny to be in my family." Poor Oliver! He backed away from the fence quickly and sat down heavily in the cold snow.

"Nobody wants me," he sobbed to himself. He covered his face with his paws and started to cry. He was so unhappy, he almost wished he was back in the animal shelter.

Suddenly a noise came from overhead.

"Psst!" it went. Oliver looked up. "Psst!" he heard again. Then he saw a scrawny cat beckoning to him from the top of a bank.

"Hey, Kitten," said the cat in a rasping voice. "You don't want to bother him, not if you know what's good for you. I heard what you said about looking for a family, and you're in the wrong place. Come with me."

The wise old cat led Oliver away from the zoo. Oliver could tell by the cat's accent that he came from the city.

"What you need, kid," said the

cat, "is a family of *HUMANS*." Oliver looked at him with surprise. "Don't worry," continued the cat whose name was Tom. "I know just the ones. I'll take you to them."

Tom knew all the tricks, and he led Oliver to a road with a row of houses. The two cats stopped outside a small house. It looked perfect. There was even a bottle of milk outside the door. The cat jumped nimbly up into a tree and walked along a branch that reached out toward the door. He pushed the bell.

There was a pause, then Oliver heard the sound of footsteps behind the door, and it swung open. A small, dark-haired girl looked out.

"Look Mum! Look Dad! It's a kitten. Oh, isn't he lovely?" The girl rushed forward and swept Oliver into her arms. "He's come to stay with us for Christmas. He's a Christmas kitten — just what I've always wanted" she cried.

"Well I never!" said her mother, and Oliver was most surprised to see the woman from the taxi. He looked around for the other cat, but he had vanished. The little girl carried Oliver inside and put him on a rug beside the fire, and her mum brought him a big bowl of milk.

"Oh, can we keep him?" asked the girl, excitedly. "You said this family needs a cat!"

"Well, yes, of course. If he wants to stay," replied her father. Oliver smiled to himself.

"Of course I want to stay," he purred. "I've got lots of grooming to catch up on."